BACK FROM THE EDGE:
STRANGE TALES FROM VALLEY FALLS

Jason Brannon

"An incredible imagination drifting the reader into the unknown world. I highly recommend escaping reality and entering into this labyrinth of mystery to uncover the supernatural elements haunting *Strange Tales from Valley Falls.*"

\- Nick Groff, EP/Host of Death Walker, Paranormal Lockdown & Ghost Adventures

ISBN: 9798563349025

This book is dedicated to the memory of Patricia Brannon, the first official member of The Deadbolt Mystery Society.

Thank you, Mom, for always believing in Shawn and me, and for teaching us to dream big. We wouldn't be where we are without your love and unending support.

TABLE OF CONTENTS

THE BEGINNING

When imagining what the command center for a ghost-hunting outfit should look like, the mind might conjure up some backwater lodge in a Louisiana bayou. In this place where communing with the dead would be expected, voodoo dolls, odd statues, and animal skulls might line the wooden shelves-the artifacts of too many strange cases to count. A Ouija board would rest in the center of an old, scarred table just waiting to be used to speak to the Other Side. A ventriloquist's dummy would probably sit in a tiny chair in one corner, taking everything in, his eyes shifting deviously every now and then (although this might be due to the fact that the floors rattle and creak whenever someone walks across them). The walls are likely covered in old Victorian cloth wallpaper that has yellowed over time, and all the lighting in the room comes from candles or oil lamps. The smell of incense would be heavy in the air.

If ever there was a place where the veil between worlds was thin, this would be it. It's a place that reeks of ectoplasm and is hazy with the ethereal remains of ghosts who are too tired to move on to the next life.

It's also a place that doesn't exist.

The HQ for the ghost-hunting group in Valley Falls known as S.T.A.L.K. (Supernatural Trackers, Annihilators, and Light Keepers) is nothing like that at all. Situated in the middle of a strip mall in the business district, S.T.A.L.K.'s inner sanctum is built more on practicality than mysticism.

On one side is a Quick Kash, where you can get a payday loan with an interest rate of around 500%—all you have to do is provide your last two pay stubs and sign over a piece of your soul. On the other side is Valley Falls Escape Rooms, where people pay to be locked in a room for an hour and forced to rely on their wits to get them out.

In the center of the two is a nondescript glass-facade suite that is home to a business that may or may not be in operation. Given the lack of decor visible through the glass, and the absence of people milling around in the lobby, it's unclear whether or not it is open or permanently closed.

Our group of ghost hunters doesn't have a neon sign on the building's facade. No card posted with business hours. No phone number to call for more information. There is no fancy window decal advertising the business name and logo. The only signs that the space is occupied by Valley Falls' preeminent group of paranormal investigators are a few vinyl letters on the front door that simply spell S.T.A.L.K.

No explanations about the group's purpose are given, and none are necessary. If you don't know what the group is about, then you don't need their help. If the problem you have requires their services, then you've already done your homework and know who they are. They don't advertise. They don't need to. You either find them, or you don't.

Over the past two years they have become very good at what they do, and their caseload has increased to the point that they are able to earn a living from their investigations. Very few paranormal groups can say that. Then again, no other group is based out of Valley Falls, a place known for its overabundance of weirdness and savagery. In this, they hold the monopoly, and more than enough strange occurrences happen inside the city limits (and in surrounding Thornmire County) to keep the S.T.A.L.K. team busy.

There are several prevailing theories about why a town the size of Valley Falls has so much bloodshed, paranormal activity, and all-around craziness that can't be neatly categorized and pigeonholed. No one, of course, has been able to prove any of said theories. All that most people know is that Valley Falls is the kind of place where the unlikely is more likely than you would think, and the inexplicable will usually remain that way, save for the occasional cases here and there solved by the Valley Falls P.D., the Will Street Detective Agency, and, of course, the good folks over at S.T.A.L.K.

S.T.A.L.K. began as four friends with a common interest in the supernatural. They started as teenagers goofing off in some of Valley Falls' oldest and creepiest homes, and their interests and skills grew with age.

Cedric's mastery of technology caused him to gravitate toward the more scientific aspects of ghost hunting, and gadgets are his domain.

Anna's long-lost grandmother was a fortune teller in The Shadow Brothers' Carnival of Chaos, and her inheritance of Madame Ruby's gift of clairvoyance made her the resident medium of the group.

Lisa spent most of her formidable years studying music theory and playing bass in a rock band in hopes of one day attending the Berkley School of Music to learn how to become a music producer. So, anything to do with audio and sound recording is her specialty.

Which leaves only Mikey, Lisa's boyfriend and resident skeptic. In the beginning, he merely went along with things because it was important to Lisa, and he used his knowledge of photography to take pictures of anything the group deemed worthy of committing to film. Over the years, his skepticism has become blunted—although not completely dulled, and he focuses on debunking the other three members' theories. Given the sorts of things that happen in Valley Falls, his record for being able to disprove the wild notions of his teammates is less than 100%. He isn't willing to say that he is wrong and that some of the strange phenomena are actually real, only that he hasn't been able to determine where he made a mistake in disproving them.

Together, they are S.T.A.L.K.

For S.T.A.L.K., the bizarre and uncanny are always on the menu, but today's special was something a bit more unusual.

They received a gift.

Without warning or explanation, the team came to possess a steamer trunk filled with the writings of a man named Lazarus Gray. They aren't sure how they came to be known by Mr. Gray, or even how the trunk found its way to their doorstep.

Lisa was the first to arrive at the office as the

5

sun was melting away into the horizon, as their days usually started in the evenings, for obvious reasons.

The trunk sat at their front door. The only reason any of them knew the identity of the trunk's owner was because his name was stenciled on one side.

For many years, Lazarus Gray told fortunes at the edge of town. He lived in a rundown trailer that looked on the verge of collapse, and he did palm readings for ten dollars each. Despite living in poverty, Lazarus Gray rubbed elbows with a lot of the movers and shakers of Valley Falls. His gift was regarded as genuine, and many influential people called on him to give them advice. He could have named his price in most cases, but he didn't because he had a personal moral code that he strictly adhered to. He charged what he felt the job was worth and not a penny more. That was one of the reasons why he garnered so much respect in the community. He wasn't your typical snake-oil salesman looking to make a quick buck off the gullibility of others. He was honest in his own way.

He was also thought by most to be The Real Deal when it came to telling the future.

Sadly, he died in his trailer a couple of weeks earlier due to complications from a brain tumor. It was a second page article in the Valley Falls Observer, and most people flipped right past it, not knowing or caring who Lazarus Gray was.

When Lisa saw the name stenciled on the trunk, she pulled it inside and wasted no time calling the other members of the group, telling them to get to the office as quickly as they could. She didn't dare risk opening it without someone else present.

By the time the other three members of S.T.A.L.K. arrived, the sun was a sliver of gold sitting precariously on the edge of the world, and the moon was climbing high into the sky. A brisk chill drifted through the air, setting a perfect mood for sorting through the possessions of a dead psychic.

Why had Lazarus Gray arranged for this trunk—filled with his belongings—to be transferred to the S.T.A.L.K. group? They didn't know the man. How did he know them? What was inside the scarred, battered box? The man had died a pauper according to all reports. Surely, there was nothing of value inside.

At half past seven, Cedric, Anna, Lisa, and Mikey stood in the back room where they usually held their meetings. A second-hand conference table sat in the center of the space, the result of a particularly fortuitous estate sale find. Posters featuring various types of weirdness adorned three of the walls: Houdini, aliens, a cryptid urban legend known as Red Fang, vampires, rock bands, Sherlock Holmes, and even a blacklight poster featuring a Cheshire cat, and the weird caterpillar from *Through the Looking Glass* smoking a hookah.

A small refrigerator hummed erratically in one corner. Sitting on top of it was a green lava lamp that cast its surroundings in an eerie extraterrestrial glow. A huge whiteboard took up most of the space on the fourth wall, and someone had taken the liberty of drawing a large purple pentagram on it in dry-erase marker. The words "Cthulhu fhtagn" had been scrawled playfully underneath.

It was as if a college dorm room and an episode of Paranormal Lockdown had a baby together.

The group congregated around the table, looking like the least likely bunch to solve any sort of case, mysterious or otherwise.

Mikey, the skeptic, stood with his arms crossed over his "I Want To Believe" t-shirt. He was a tall, lanky guy with brown hair and a wispy moustache.

By contrast, Cedric—who was more solidly built and dark-haired—was fiddling with his smartwatch. The skull watch face he had installed wasn't to his liking, and he was busy changing it out with an image of a creepy eyeball instead.

Anna, a blonde petite girl with a glow that was equal parts beauty and aura, stood there in her Florence and the Machine shirt, listening to something on her ear pods, moving her head to the unheard music. In all likelihood, because of her gift, she was more acutely attuned to the situation than anyone else in the room, even though it seemed that her attentions were divided.

Of the four of them, Lisa was the only one who was intently focused on the trunk. Although the group didn't have an official leader, she was usually the one to get things done and get people moving in the right direction. She even looked the part. Raven-haired, dark-eyed, exotic, and wearing just a hint of darkness, Lisa was the mysterious kind of girl who could serve as the face of an equally mysterious group that researched places and events.

"Why are we here, Lisa?" Mikey asked his girlfriend. "I didn't think we had any active cases at the moment."

"I told you," Lisa said as she pulled her dark hair back into a ponytail, preparing to open the trunk. "I got here and found this weird old trunk sitting at the front door. It belonged to Lazarus Gray. Pretty cool, huh?"

"Who is Lazarus Gray?" he asked.

"He was a local mystic. People claimed that he saw things in visions. I think he helped the Valley Falls P.D. a few times with missing persons cases."

"So what do any of those things have to do

with us?" Mikey asked.

"That's what we're going to find out," Lisa replied. "By the way, who peed in your Cheerios today?"

Mikey sighed and stuffed his hands into his jean pockets. "I don't mean to be in a mood. It's just hard for me to get as excited as you do about this stuff. I'm immediately suspicious when a strange trunk is left on our doorstep by someone we don't know and have never met."

Lisa nodded. "You're right. It's weird. But it's a mysterious box from Lazarus Gray! How is that not exciting?"

"Nobody but me finds this all a little suspect?" Mikey asked. He pulled a cigarette case out of his pocket, selected one, and put it in his mouth. But he didn't light it. It was a habit that helped him think. He never actually smoked the cigarettes. Not any more at least.

"Of course we do," Cedric replied, still fiddling with his watch. "But this could be a big deal. Lazarus Gray was one of the most well-regarded psychics around these parts. Don't be such a buzzkill."

"I get the feeling that we're going to want to open that chest and see what's inside," Anna said as she removed her earbuds. "Something tells me that Mr. Gray might have brought us something extremely important."

"Because you sense it?" Mikey said playfully.

Anna just nodded, remaining quiet. Of the four of them, she was the most withdrawn usually.

"Ok, fine," Mikey sighed. "I'll shut up so we can get down to business."

"Finally," Lisa said with a grin. "Any objection to me cracking this thing open and seeing what's inside?"

There were no objections.

With a flick of her wrists, the latches on the old trunk were flipped back, and the lid was opened. Inside, the trunk was filled with various old moth-eaten journals and yellowed notebooks.

A note addressed to them sat at the very top of the heap.

It read as follows:

Dear members of S.T.A.L.K.,

My name is Lazarus Gray, and if you're reading this letter then I am dead. I left specific instructions to have the contents of this trunk delivered to you in the event of my passing on this very specific day, because within the next twenty-four hours a tragedy will occur somewhere in Valley Falls. I hope you will be able to stop it from happening.

You don't know me, but I've seen you at work quite a few times when I slipped out of my body at night and went walking around the dark streets and shadow-filled places of town as I'm prone to do in my astral state. As a result, I'm convinced you're the group for the job at hand. The things I've seen have only impressed upon me how formidable a team you are and have helped me make the decision to leave the entirety of my work to the four of you.

You've already helped quite a few people with your gifts and talents, and helping people is what I tried to do with my gifts as well. People in Valley Falls need all the help they can get, as I'm sure you've seen firsthand; and you will need help as well. Valley Falls is a place like no other. There are reasons for that, but I won't go into them here. What I've left you is the thing that will help you most: information."

"As you may or may not know, I have been diagnosed with an inoperable brain tumor. In my condition, there are times when it becomes difficult to separate fantasy from reality. Most of these stories are works of fancy conjured up by my ailing mind. Which one is real, I do not know. But my gift is doing its best to shine through, and I believe that one of the stories in this volume will become a self-fulfilling prophecy unless you intervene. Each of the books in this trunk, in fact, has one story that will come true. Those books are all dated weeks or months in the future. The book on top is dated today which is why the trunk was delivered to you now. There is no time to waste. You can actually prevent one of these terrible things from occurring. You can save lives and do some good. Nobody else besides you would even entertain such a notion. But you are an open-minded *lot. You have to be. Your work requires it."*

*"Most of the accounts you will read are on the unbeliev-
able side, but then again, Valley Falls is the type of place
where the unbelievable happens almost daily. You will need
the knowledge that I've gained over the years to find out
what's true and what's not. So read the tales I have provided
in my journals and use that knowledge to help the citizens
of Valley Falls. Consider this a gift from a friend. And
while I'm dead, that doesn't mean we can't talk every now
and then. You hunt ghosts for a living. I'm sure you'll figure
out how to contact me if you need to talk.*

"Until then, Lazarus."

With the conclusion of the letter, the four
members of the group looked at each other with
uncertainty.

"So, one of the stories in this book is going to
come true and people will die unless we prevent it?"
Cedric said, completely forgetting about his watch
now. "No pressure there. Couldn't he have given us
a heads up or something? Maybe have it delivered
yesterday so we could have more time to think?"

"If he had given us too much time, we might
have talked ourselves into doubting the whole
thing," Anna said. "By dumping it into our laps,
Lazarus Gray is forcing us to act because there isn't
time to do enough research to prove or disprove

13

its validity."

"How do we even take this seriously?" Mikey asked. "This is crazy even for us, and we investigate hauntings."

"How can we not take it seriously?" Anna said. "If there is a chance that someone in this town is going to die and we could prevent it, we have to treat Lazarus Gray's account as credible."

"Even if it sounds crazy?" Mikey said.

"Especially if it sounds crazy," Lisa reminded him. "That's the kind of place we live in."

"Am I the only one with a bad feeling about this?" Mikey asked.

"No." Cedric spoke up. "I don't like it either. I like making my own decisions and not feeling as though I'm being forced into something. This feels like I don't really have a choice. I don't like it, but I agree with Anna. We have to check it out."

"Fine," Mikey said. "We better start reading. Lisa, you do it. You have a good speaking voice."

"OK, Mr. Bossy Pants," Lisa said playfully as she took the topmost book out of the trunk and opened it to the first page. "Back from the Edge: Strange Tales From Valley Falls, by Lazarus Gray," she said.

And with that, she began to read aloud a series of strange (and possibly true) tales of a town that had more secrets than most...

14

BEWARE THE
DEATH ANGEL

Heaps of dead leaves lined the streets of Valley Falls. Scarecrows, crudely fashioned out of broomsticks and old clothing, stood watch over the neighborhood. Fake spider-webbing clung to the foundations of each house like a fine layer of graveyard mist. White garbage bags filled with confetti had been made to look like ghosts floating above each roof. Stray strands of toilet paper dangled from a tree here and there—the remnants of teenage mischief. There was no denying that this was October country.

Wallace piloted his Buick through streets like the ferryman's skiff through black waters. He kept waiting for his headlights to outline the small moving shape of a superhero or ballerina or a zombie with a meat cleaver buried in its head, but there didn't seem to be any kids out yet.

He checked his watch. Nearly 7:30. Weird.

He turned off on the boulevard, hoping to

dodge as much Halloween traffic as possible. Above all else, he didn't want to get trapped in a convoy of mini-vans. That didn't seem to be a problem. The street was deserted, but it was far from empty.

Although they had lived in this town for a month now, Wallace still hadn't gotten used to the way people in the South piled their trash at the edge of the street. Normally they just put out the customary bags of garbage in black bags. Tonight, however, the people of Valley Falls had put out everything but the kitchen sink…and upon closer inspection there were even one or two of those as well.

Old freezers, rusty wagons, wheelbarrows, galvanized metal buckets, trash cans, and a few discolored Igloo ice chests flanked either side of the blacktop. Wallace hadn't lived here long enough to know if tomorrow was pick-up day or not. Still, it seemed like an abnormal amount of junk.

He was thinking about how much he disliked this backwoods community when his cell phone rang. The unexpectedness of the call made him jump. He didn't have to look at the I.D. to know it was Martha. She was the only one who knew his number. For that matter, she was probably the only one in this hick town who even knew how to operate a cell phone.

"Joe's Pool Hall," he said gruffly into the telephone. "Eight-Ball speaking."

"Stop playing. I need you to do me a favor," Martha said.

Wallace sighed. "I'm tired, sweetheart. I had a mess to deal with at work. Can't I just come home to you for a while?"

"We don't have any candy," Martha said, unsympathetic to her husband's problems. "I need you to go to the store and pick some up. This is our first Halloween in town."

"I'm tired," Wallace repeated. "I don't really want to see any kids. Most of 'em probably don't have teeth anyway. This is the South, remember?"

"I'm from the South," Martha said firmly. "You didn't seem to have any problems with me when we first met. I wasn't barefoot, clad in overalls, and snaggle-toothed."

"No," Wallace sighed, remembering the sight of her on the day they met. "You weren't. But that's beside the point. Do I really have to go to the store before coming home?"

"I'll give you a kiss for each piece of candy you bring home. And if you're good, maybe you'll get a treat at the end of the night instead of a trick."

Wallace smiled. He hated the way she could manipulate him sometimes.

Knowing it was useless to put off the inevitable, he turned the Buick around and headed to the market.

Given that it was Halloween, he hoped the store would be deserted so he could make his purchase and run. But the parking lot was packed with people.

Disgusted after several minutes of circling the lot in search of a spot, Wallace had to park on the other side of the street and walk to the store. Once inside, he recognized a few faces, but didn't know anybody's name. Everyone seemed to stare at him with curiosity before turning their attention back to the meat counter, where the majority of the customers were gathered.

Wallace snarled at the hicks. He hated this town.

As he walked up and down the aisles, he noticed that the shelves of Halloween candy were surprisingly full. Nobody seemed to give a rip about treating the children to a mouthful of cavities. They were more interested in what the butcher had to offer and were congregated around the meat counter. The townspeople all looked like they were getting ready for a cookout, buying ribs and cutlets and sirloins and roasts. Strangely enough, the shelves with charcoal and lighter fluid were full too.

Wallace supposed there might be some sort of tradition in the town that he hadn't heard about, a

Halloween festival or something. But the stern, worried expressions on each face made him think otherwise. These people didn't look like they were preparing for a good time. Instead, they wore the masks of mourners picking out graveside flowers in a florist's shop.

"OK, folks," the ruddy-faced butcher behind the counter said, "I'm down to a ribeye and three pounds of hamburger."

A gangly man wearing a grease-stained work shirt stepped up to the counter. "I'll take it all."

The groans of disapproval from the crowd were immediate.

"You don't need that much, Luke," an old woman wearing a pillbox hat spoke up. "One pound of hamburger will suffice. What will the rest of us do come nightfall?"

"I don't care," Luke replied, slamming his money down on the counter as the butcher hesitantly wrapped all the meat in white paper. "Better to be safe than sorry."

Like the Pied Piper, Luke left the store with at least a dozen people muttering and shuffling along behind him. Curious, Wallace followed them.

"I'll give you $50 for that ribeye," one man said as the mob surrounded Luke.

"Seventy-five," another spoke up.

The little old woman with the pillbox hat quickly rifled through her purse. She pulled out a wad of fives and tens and counted it with the skill and ease of a bank teller. "A hundred and five is all I've got," she said. "Sell it to me."

Luke, seeing an opportunity to make a little profit, sold the ribeye and began systematically auctioning off the other two pounds of hamburger he'd just bought. He kept only one pound of hamburger for himself. Puzzled by the whole thing, Wallace headed back inside to the meat counter, eager to understand what was going on.

"What is the big deal?" he asked the butcher. "You sell out like this every day?"

The butcher wiped his greasy hands on his blood-stained apron and leaned over the counter. "Not everyday. Just on Halloween. Today's special. Always has been."

"And why is that?" Wallace asked. Suddenly, all he wanted to do was to pick up Martha's bag of candy and get home to his recliner.

"The Death Angel's coming tonight," the butcher said cryptically. "You'd do well to beware."

"Fine. If you don't want to let the new guy in on the secret, that's ok with me. You don't have to patronize."

"I'm serious," the butcher said, leaning over

the counter to whisper his caveat. "Beware the Death Angel." Something about the way he looked at Wallace made him realize the man truly believed what he was saying.

"All I came in here for is some Halloween candy for the kids," Wallace said, picking up a bag of bite-sized Snickers. "I'll just pay for this and leave you alone. You've obviously had a stressful day."

"You'll need more than candy," the butcher said. "The Death Angel needs flesh and blood. He'll get it one way or the other. If you don't leave something for him, he'll take what he wants. You may not be happy with that outcome."

Outside, visible through the front window of the store, a fight had erupted over the last pound of hamburger meat. Two mechanics were slugging it out like prize-fighters. Apparently, they believed in the Death Angel just as much as the butcher. Wallace wasn't buying it. It was probably some hill-billy trick these inbreds were playing on him because he was from the city.

"You'd better leave something for The Death Angel," the butcher said as Wallace headed to his car. "Otherwise, this may be the first and last time we meet."

"Only if I'm lucky," Wallace muttered as he got in his Buick. Chunks of raw hamburger clung to his windshield like slugs, sliding slowly down the glass and leaving a slick spot in their wake. The remnants of that last pound of hamburger meat lay on the sidewalk. Obviously, both men had been so determined to get the meat for themselves that they had torn the package. Still, it looked like a lot of the meat had been scooped up and carried away. Ants had started to claim what was left.

Cursing, Wallace turned on his wipers and shot some washer fluid onto the glass. It just made a bigger mess. But after several minutes the windshield was clear enough to see through. Wallace threw the Buick in reverse and headed home.

Unlike before, there were people on the streets, but they weren't trick-or-treating. They were carrying the meat they had purchased to the edge of the road, dumping it into the wagons, ice chests, buckets, and old freezers that Wallace had mistakenly confused for junk.

Although it was foolish, the scene reminded him of those days long ago when he would spend a week with his grandfather on the farm. They had done something very similar when filling the troughs with animal feed.

"The Death Angel," Wallace muttered to himself. "You can tell we're living in the Bible Belt. Wait until Martha hears about this."

But Martha was busy dragging Wallace's massive toolbox out to the side of the road.

"What are you doing?" Wallace asked, slamming the car door. "That's my toolbox you're scraping against the ground."

"I know you're going to think I'm crazy, but I've got something to tell you."

"The Death Angel?" he asked.

"You heard it too, then?"

"You're not going to tell me you believe it, are you?"

Martha looked at Wallace sternly. "It's just a little raw meat, Wallace. It's not like we'd be throwing our life's savings out the window. The story might be true, and it might not be. But it's a small price to pay for safety."

"We're not doing it. Put my toolbox back where it was. I don't want a bunch of maggots crawling around in it before I even get to use it once."

Martha was a small, mousy woman with brown hair and simple features who seemed mild-mannered at first glance. Yet, Wallace's reaction galvanized her. She stood up straight and glared at her husband. "I'm leaving it where it is. I'll buy you a new one tomorrow," she said curtly.

"Absolutely not. This is ridiculous."

Martha's pale blue eyes burned with cold fire.

She took a deep breath to steady herself, and the fire in her eyes died a little bit. "Wallace, for once could you just go along with what I want to do? Even if it seems foolish. Please?"

Wallace sighed and shrugged his shoulders. "Do whatever you want. You usually do anyway. Here's your candy."

Martha took the bag of Snickers and walked back toward the house.

"Oh, there's one more thing," Wallace said with obvious satisfaction. "I ate the last steak yesterday while you were out job hunting. And I can't go and buy any more because the market is sold out. So, I guess you won't be able to do what you want after all."

"What are we going to do?" Martha asked, suddenly fearful.

"We're going to live our lives like we always do and prove to these honky-tonk bumpkins that they're wasting their time."

"Why don't we just get in the car and go somewhere nice tonight," Martha said. "Maybe go into Crowley's Point and catch a horror flick for Halloween. Then we could rent a hotel room and enjoy ourselves. It would be so spontaneous. Not at all like the routine we normally lead."

Wallace could feel his face turning red. "We're not

doing that because there's no reason to. We're not leaving our home because the citizens of Mayberry think the boogeyman's coming out tonight."

Livid, Martha stomped back inside. Wallace thought about moving his toolbox and then decided to wait until after he'd eaten supper. He was hungry. The toolbox could wait.

Martha didn't say much during their meal. The doorbell didn't ring either despite Martha leaving the porch light on to hopefully attract a few sugar-hungry children. The unopened bag of Snickers sat in a kettle by the door.

"It's odd, isn't it?" Wallace said, trying to break through Martha's icy mood. "No children trick-or-treating on Halloween night."

"The town's scared," Martha said firmly. "No parent in their right mind would let their kids go out when something dangerous is skulking around the neighborhoods."

"OK, let's cut through all this superstitious garbage. How did you find out about all of this in the first place?"

"The Jacksons next door. I saw Tina dragging an old washtub out to the side of the road. I went to help her and asked what she was doing. That's when she told me about the Death Angel."

"And everything that Tina Jackson says is absolutely 100% true?" Wallace said before filling his mouth with a spoonful of mashed potatoes. "You've only known this woman a couple of weeks. She could be a paranoid schizophrenic or something. You don't know."

"I believe her," Martha said grimly. "She said the Death Angel took one of her kids. She even showed me pictures of the little girl. Blonde hair. Green eyes. Pigtails. Missing since October 31st, three years ago. That was the year the Jacksons moved here."

"Why didn't they pack up their stuff and leave after the Death Angel took their child?"

"They thought she might have been kidnapped by one of the local rednecks and hoped they would get her back. Still do, I guess. Moving away would be a sign of giving up. Even now, I'm not sure they completely believe in the Death Angel. But it's the explanation everyone else uses when rationalizing the girl's disappearance."

"This town is strange," Wallace said, shaking his head. "We're moving away from here the first chance we get. Tomorrow, in fact. I can't stand the thought of living here."

"Let's be reasonable," Martha pleaded. "We haven't given this place a chance yet."

"Because it doesn't deserve one," Wallace

fumed, backing away from the dinner table.

They didn't say anything to each other for the next couple of hours. Wallace watched an old John Wayne movie on TV. Martha busied herself with cleaning up the kitchen and washing a few loads of clothes. Neither of them mentioned the Death Angel, although it was apparent that *The Sands of Iwo Jima* and dirty socks were the last things on their minds.

When they went to bed, Wallace faced one wall and Martha faced the other. There was more distance than love between them that night.

"11:40," Wallace muttered, looking at the clock before shutting his eyes. "Seven o'clock is going to come early in the morning."

Martha didn't reply.

The icy silence between them was broken at eleven-fifty, when the screaming started.

At first Wallace wasn't even sure he'd heard it. It was only as he sat up in bed and saw that Martha was awake too that he knew it was real.

"It's just somebody playing a Halloween prank or maybe one of those haunted house soundtracks with all the screaming and rattling chains."

"You know it isn't," Martha said. Even in the dark, Wallace could see how pale her face had become. She was trembling.

Wallace threw the comforter back and

stumbled over to the window. Looking out, he couldn't see anything. But the noises outside grew louder. Trash cans and galvanized buckets were being knocked over. The noise was akin to the sound of a baseball bat smashing against a metal mailbox.

"Dogs," Wallace said. "Just a pack of strays out there trying to get at the meat everyone's been putting out. Or raccoons maybe. It's bound to happen. Let's go back to bed."

"I can't sleep with all that's going on," Martha said, slipping into her housecoat. "I've got to find something to put out and quick."

Before Wallace could protest, she was already bounding down the stairs, heading for the kitchen. When he finally caught up to her, she was throwing icy bags of peas and carrots out of the freezer.

"What on earth are you doing?" he asked her.

Martha whirled on him. "I don't have time to argue with you. The Death Angel will be here soon. I think there may be a bag of frozen pork chops up here somewhere."

"Will you get hold of yourself?" Wallace growled, grabbing Martha by the arm to drag her away from the refrigerator.

She pulled away and began hurling ice trays across the kitchen in an attempt to unearth any stray scrap of meat that she might have missed.

"Martha, stop!" Wallace shouted, more worried than angry now. He'd never seen his wife act like this, and it scared him.

But Martha didn't stop, and neither did the screaming from up the street. Only when the freezer was completely empty, and the refrigerator's shelves were bare, did Martha allow herself to rest.

Wallace wasn't sure how to proceed, but he did the only thing he knew. He kissed Martha on top of her head and pulled her close to him. "Things will be fine," he told her. "Just give it a little time. It will be morning before you know it."

"I wonder how many people won't be around to see morning," Martha said.

Wallace suddenly couldn't help himself. She was being foolish, and he was tired of it. One way or another, he was going to knock this lunacy out of her head. "I don't want to hear another word about this," he shouted, holding Martha at arm's length.

"Then go upstairs," she told him firmly.

And that was it. Wallace had had enough. He grabbed her firmly by the wrist. "Let's go," he growled. "We're going to go outside and prove to you that there isn't anything to be afraid of."

"No," Martha screamed, frantic.

But Wallace was stronger. Because Martha's house shoes gave her very little traction on the linoleum, she slid across the floor. Wallace didn't stop pulling.

"Let's go and see the Death Angel," he said. "This should prove once and for all just how paranoid and backwoods this town is."

Martha, however, had other ideas. She managed to grab one of the fireplace implements as Wallace dragged her toward the door. Before he could raise a hand to block her attack, Martha clubbed him in the back of the head. Wallace went down hard, immediately releasing his grip on his wife.

* * *

Wallace opened his eyes slowly, unsure of where he was at first. It was dark, and he seemed to be stuck in some sort of hole. But that wasn't entirely right either as he realized that he was sitting in his oversized toolbox. Martha had knocked him out and somehow managed to drag him out here. His hands and feet were bound with duct tape.

He could feel the rage building in him and struggled frantically to free himself from the work box. She had thrown him out with the belief that the Death Angel would take him instead of her, and it infuriated him. One, because she had bought into the whole nonsense. Two, because it showed how selfish she really was.

Wallace stopped struggling when he heard Mrs. Olson from two houses down sobbing uncontrollably.

"Please don't take Charlie," she pleaded. "He's all I've got. I put out a pot roast for you. Honest, I did. Someone must have stolen it."

And then the lamentations started afresh.

Wallace strained to see who she was talking to, but all he could see was a dark furtive shape like smoke, a hazy black mist hovering around the empty toy wagon. Then the smoke began to clear. A pair of strong, translucent wings materialized from the smog. They were attached to a muscular frame made of black leather. Strong legs, powerful torso, arms that ended not in hands but in talons. A demon's face with a masochist's smile. White fangs tinted red. Yellow eyes. Two small spiraling horns ending in sharp points. A fallen angel in every sense of the word. It looked like something out of Gustave Dore's depictions of Hell.

The Death Angel smiled at Wallace and headed in his direction.

"No," he muttered to himself as he tried to free his hands and feet.

The Death Angel came closer, morphing into black fog that crept and swirled along the ground.

It was like watching a brewing thunderhead form and churn.

"Martha!" Wallace screamed, hoping his wife would come to her senses and help him. But Martha made no move to come out of the house.

Wallace craned his neck to search for her and saw her worried face staring back at him from one of the upstairs windows. She quickly pulled the curtains shut, unwilling to watch what was about to happen to her husband.

Thankfully, the Death Angel was methodical and stopped one house down. Wallace tried to stand up and hop toward the house. But Martha had been thorough with the way she bound him. He managed to wriggle out of the toolbox only to fall flat on his face in the lawn. The grass was wet and moist against his cheek.

"Martha!" he screamed. But the light in the upstairs room went off. Like a frightened turtle, Martha wasn't sticking her head out until she was certain the coast was clear.

Wallace managed to turn himself over, and watched in horror as the dark creature stuck its slanted head into what might have been a feeding trough and began to eat the raw meat. For a moment or two there was only the ripping of animal flesh and the smacking of black lips.

Then Wallace saw the Death Angel lift its head and look at him once again. He could tell by the way it bared its teeth that it was smiling. He opened his mouth to scream when he heard something behind him. It was Martha with a pair of scissors.

"Hurry," Wallace implored, watching the beast as it stalked him. Martha held up the scissors as the dark fog swirled around them. "I should have listened to you," Wallace said, trembling. "I'm sorry. Now cut me loose."

"Oh, I didn't come out here to cut you loose," Martha said, keeping her eyes focused on the obsidian figure striding toward them. "I came here to make sure that it takes you instead of me."

"What do you mean?" Wallace asked, horrified. "Let me go."

"The Death Angel passes over the houses that offer it flesh and blood. I've taken care of the flesh part. Now for the blood..."

Wallace screamed as Martha buried the scissors into his thigh. Immediately, crimson streams jettisoned into the air.

The Death Angel moved faster.

Wallace, seizing his only chance, lunged out at Martha with his bound feet. The kick hit her in the center of the chest, pushing her toward the beast. The Death Angel caught her and buried its teeth into her throat. The scream was short-lived, becoming little more than a watery gurgle.

Wallace cried out as he watched his wife fall to the ground. Most of her throat was gone, and her eyes had the faraway look of a Hypnos addict after taking a hit. It wasn't supposed to happen like this. But a split second of panic had changed everything.

And still the Death Angel moved forward. Wallace trembled as it stood before him, its mouth painted with Martha's blood. He closed his eyes, waiting for the moment when it ripped his head away from his shoulders to get at the hot blood within. But that never happened. Instead, it moved quietly on to the next house. Martha had been sacrifice enough to save Wallace's life, and he felt sick at the thought of what he had done. He had given his own partner over to the Death Angel, and he lived as a result.

Yes, she had tied him up with the intent of offering him to the beast. But her mind had been clouded by fear, by the certainty that she was going to die if she didn't do something quickly. The worst thing about it was that she hadn't resorted to that immediately. She had wanted to put some meat out like everyone else had done. Wallace had been the one to squash that idea. Now his wife was gone.

The more he thought about it all the sicker he

felt. He thought about all of the good times he and Martha had shared and then thought of the bloody way she had left this earth. Suddenly, it was too much to bear. He hobbled over to one of the flower beds and promptly threw up in the rose bushes. His throat burned, and his mouth carried the bitter taste of stomach acid.

Once he was done being sick, Wallace took several deep breaths and walked around the yard, feeling utterly lost and alone.

So much had gone wrong in such a short amount of time. Emotions had flared, and bad decisions had been made. Now, there was only the grisly, traumatic aftermath left to deal with. The thought of what had happened saddened and enraged Wallace. He thought he understood why the Jacksons hadn't moved away yet. Maybe they realized what had taken their daughter and were simply unwilling to let her death go unavenged.

If only Martha hadn't been so stupid. She had tried to kill him! She had forced him to defend herself! What a mess she had made. This was her fault. But he also blamed himself.

Despite their differences, and the throbbing ache in his thigh where Martha had buried the scissors, Wallace had loved his wife and knew that her reactions had been the direct result of her fear. It saddened him to think that he could have prevented it all with a simple pork chop or a pound of raw hamburger. Or by simply taking her to the movies in the next town as she'd suggested.

Before, he had been ready to leave Valley Falls as quickly as possible. Now, he wasn't sure he would ever leave. If need be, he would stay as many Halloweens as it took until he found the creature's weakness. Then, he would kill it.

He raked his wrists along the rough edge of the toolbox until the duct tape frayed and eventually tore enough that he could free himself. Then, after pulling the scissors out of his thigh, he staggered back to the house, where he bandaged himself up.

Then Wallace pulled up a lawn chair and sat out on his porch, listening to the wailing of families up and down the street who hadn't heeded the warnings. He cried right along with them until the sun came up.

FOLLOW THE LEADER

I like to walk late at night. It's a good way to unwind after a stressful day of listening to the whispering machines, to the singing cogs, to the screaming gears turning and locking into place. Evidently, lots of other people like to walk at night too, although I didn't realize it until my insomnia forced me out into the streets of my town at a little past one in the morning.

Walking helps give my life structure, and that's exactly what I need. There's something very routine and methodical about putting one foot in front of the other. It's almost mechanical how all the parts function together—the heart beating, legs pumping, lungs bellowing air. Strange that I should liken the body to a machine after all I've been through. Old habits die hard, I guess.

The machines hadn't spoken to me in a little over six months, and I was beginning to think that I was in control of my life again. I had a good job building furniture. I paid my bills on time. I did all my own grocery shopping. I had even gone on a date or two with women who knew nothing of my past.

Six months ago, while listening to the chit-chat of microchips, I would have never dreamed that this sort of life was possible. Of course, to most people, this sort of life isn't that extraordinary. I might have agreed with them had I not spent most of my days and nights with plugs in my ears trying to block out the whirring binary voices of the machines around me that were continually urging me to do unspeakable things.

I'm certain that the nocturnal strolls around the block helped insulate me against the noise. Being outside in the open air was like an inoculation against the hum of microwaves, the buzz of free-flowing electricity, and the screech of unoiled mechanisms. That Tuesday I needed all the help I could get. My head was filled to overflowing with harsh sounds, whispers, and the chuffing of un-greased pistons.

After finishing my walk and clearing my head of all the electronic debris that had collected there during the day, I took a quick shower, jumped into my pajamas, and readied myself for bed.

I sighed, pushed back the covers, and got out of bed moments after getting in it. I read for a few minutes, drank warm milk, put my ear plugs in so

I could watch an infomercial on TV without fear of suggestion, and even considered counting sheep. But nothing helped.

I decided to go for another walk.

This time, when I ventured out of the house, the temperature had dropped a little. The moon had shifted in the sky, and the heavens lit up at irregular intervals with brief bursts of lightning.

Oblivious to everything but the night around him, a man stood on the corner, tapping his foot impatiently like he was waiting for someone.

Dressed entirely in black, the man stared at me with equal parts amusement and curiosity. He only stood there a few seconds before motioning for me to follow him. Then he turned and walked away.

I think the gears inside my watch were making sounds not unlike human speech, nudging me to break free of my strait-jacket routine and follow the man. As I had done so many times before, I listened to the voices and pursued him.

My curiosity grew as I saw other people standing on the street corners and then subsequently falling in behind us like Hamelin rats. By the time we had gone a few blocks, there were seven of us. The rest of the group eyed me carefully but said nothing. No doubt they were wondering who I was. I had the same question about them.

I started to speak when the man I was following held a finger up to his lips in a quieting gesture. "Not now," he whispered. "We'll talk later."

Our destination was a two-story Victorian that had seen better days, but still somehow managed to stand despite a cracked foundation and rampant evidence of termites. No lights burned in any of the windows, and it was logical to assume that everyone inside was asleep. Our guide motioned for us to follow him as he tiptoed up to the porch. I felt myself slipping into old habits. This is how it had started before, with the clocks commanding me, the radios urging me onward, the satellites in space spurning me into action.

Our leader tried the front door only to find it locked. He wasted no time pulling out a set of picks. Within seconds the lock was sprung, and the door swung open with a quiet hiss.

I entered the house, feeling like some sleeping part of me was about to wake up. Imagine the confusion on my face when I saw the leader reach into one of his pockets and pull out a handful of those unfurling noise makers that are so popular with kids at birthday parties. This derailed every expectation I had up this point. I had anticipated guns or knives or shackles, not children's toys.

Somehow, all seven of us managed to creep up

to the second floor without waking anyone. Our leader smiled and pointed to one of the rooms. The door was closed but not locked. Inside, an elderly man and woman slept peacefully while a ceiling fan turned in lazy circles. The digital clock beside their bed read 1:16 in bright bold letters. I think it said something to me, but I was too busy trying to understand what was going on to listen.

"On three," our leader whispered as he placed the party whistle up to his lips. He performed the countdown with his fingers, holding up one, then two, and finally three. We all blew on our noise makers at the same time.

The old man and woman jumped up—confused, frightened, and disoriented. The woman screamed as she saw all of us in her bedroom. The man, more angry than shocked, fumbled around in a drawer, eventually producing a chrome-handled pistol that gleamed in the moonlight. The sight of that gun was all we needed to send us running down the stairs and out of the house.

The old man fired at us a couple of times from his front porch, but missed. Once safely on the street again, everyone went their separate directions, except for me and my guide.

He followed me long enough to explain what I had gotten myself involved in. "We do this every night. A different one of us is always in charge. We never know what kind of situation we'll find ourselves in. It's always up to the leader, and that's the fun of it. None of us know each other either, and that's probably for the best. Come out tomorrow at the same time. And this time, wear black. Nobody comes with you either."

I didn't get a chance to ask any questions as the leader of the group ran away into the shadows, leaving me with a sense of exhilaration I hadn't felt in many, many years. It was exactly the sort of feeling I had gotten when the machines spoke to me for the first time.

I spent the next day thinking about what the following night might hold, and debating on whether or not I should go out again. Of course, there was no real possibility that I would back out.

The next evening, I set my alarm clock to wake me at ten minutes until one. The clock screamed at me just as intended, promising me a night of exhilaration, and I woke up feeling invigorated.

The group was out in force. This time we were led by a buxom redhead dressed in dark coveralls. I definitely hadn't seen her the night before. I would have remembered.

I had taken the advice and dressed in black. There were nine of us that evening, and at least half of the walkers were new...or new to me. I wondered how many people in this town were privy to these late-night jaunts, and how many of these faces I would recognize at the bank or the grocery store or the gas station.

We went in a completely different direction from the night before, making twists and turns through the streets that were unfamiliar to me. I didn't start to get anxious and jittery until we left the sanctuary of sidewalks and brightly lit streets and headed down a winding trail that branched off through a patch of dark woods.

I paused for a moment when we reached the cemetery. Shovels were lined up single-file against the wrought iron gates. Moonlight trickled through the trees.

"Grab a shovel," our leader said. It was a command I had heard before when all the machines in my house decided to put in their two cents worth. Of course, that was long before the blood and the screaming and the jail time.

Our leader threw her shovel over the gate and scaled it with the agility of a cat. We followed suit and marched single file through the labyrinth of graves. We were nearly at the back of the cemetery when our leader abruptly stopped and plunged her shovel into the soft earth covering someone named

"Maggie Lynn, Devoted Mother."

Nobody else seemed to give a second thought to what we were doing. They all dug with reckless abandon, flinging dirt aside and keeping their attention focused on the job at hand. I couldn't help looking over my shoulder every now and then out of fear that the police would step out of nowhere and cuff us all. I guess I was just paranoid. People who hear voices usually are.

With nine of us digging, it didn't take very long to reach the coffin. I knew we weren't going to just stop with unearthing the casket. We were going to open it.

Strangely, it felt like I had gone back in time.

The body had been interred for quite a while. Long enough, in fact, to make the exhumation more pleasant than I would have expected. The corpse wasn't icky and wet like I thought it would be. Rather, it was dried, withered, and shrunken like a mummy in a floral print dress.

"Everybody take a souvenir," the redhead instructed.

The deceased had obviously been a lover of jewelry and had a ring for each finger. One for each of us. The redhead, however, wasn't content with a tarnished trinket. Although I didn't see what she took, I heard something crackle that sounded like a stick being snapped in half. I wanted to do as our leader had done, but I was afraid that taking such a gruesome souvenir might be the very thing that pushed me back into a world of savagery and madness. In the end, I settled for a ring like everybody else. That night, I slept with it under my pillow.

I was elected to be the leader the next night, and I had absolutely no idea what I was going to do. It was so much easier to be a follower. Leading took work and planning. To make matters more complicated, I couldn't blame any of the voices on the machines anymore. The machines weren't the ones speaking to me. In fact, I was certain they never had. The voices were all mine.

I called in sick at my job the following day and spent the afternoon wondering what kind of excursion I could devise. The night's festivities needed to be exciting, a little bit dangerous, and quite possibly illegal. After spending several hours thinking, I came up with just the thing. Or rather the voices came up with it and I listened to them.

Ever since that first walk, I had wondered what possessed these people to follow their leader without regard for any sense of morality or legality. But the deeper I delved, the more I realized that this entire game was built on trust. That was what made it exciting, the Not Knowing. To put their fate into the hands of someone they didn't even know was their form of exhilaration, of recreation. It was their way of getting high. These were the sorts of people who thrived on jumping out of airplanes, of bungee jumping, of eating rare and exotic foods, of getting in the car and driving with no clear destination in mind. These were thrill seekers searching for that new rush, and tonight they were expecting me to provide that.

No one questioned me as we trudged along the highway that wound up to the cliff's peak. Most of them had been there in the past when making out with old lovers in the backseat of a car.

The cliff was deserted when we reached the top, but it was obvious from the looks on everyone's faces that they were familiar with the place.

No one questioned me as I handed out the blindfolds. "Put these on," I told them.

"What I want everyone to do is simple," I said. "This little nighttime organization is built on trust and the possibility of a cheap thrill. It's also based on following the leader. I want to see just how far you'll take it. Basically, I want everyone to keep your blindfolds on and follow the sound of my voice."

There was a bit of murmuring, but everyone participated. I led them in circles at first, winding in and out of the long rows of wild brush that flanked either side of the cliff. Once I was sure no one knew exactly where they were in relation to the cliff face, I chose a spot on an outcropping of rock and beckoned the group to me.

Like lemmings, they followed. And like nighttime stars, they fell. Not one of them screamed.

They lay there at the bottom like that for a very long time. When I was sure none of them were still alive, I headed back home, feeling a little like Jim Jones. These people had gone to their deaths because of something I told them to do. I felt like a god.

I went home and went to sleep immediately. I didn't dream. I didn't toss and turn. In fact, I slept better than I have in quite a while. I was still drunk on power then.

I woke up refreshed and invigorated and looking forward to the night's festivities. The new leader might ask me to walk blindly off the edge of a cliff to my death. That was what made this so exciting and what made me tingle every time I thought of the myriad possibilities.

Whatever the case, I would follow willingly and do as I was told. I was prepared for anything now.

I couldn't wait until it was my turn to be leader again.

Neither could the voices...

I'LL BE HERE AT MIDNIGHT

Amir was a fraud. The higher ups at the Shadow Brothers' Carnival of Chaos, he suspected, knew he had no psychic gifts. He couldn't interpret a hand of Tarot, or read lifelines, or see into past lives. He had been hired to do the job after Madame Ruby—the last fortune teller—was murdered by one of the carnies.

Although the job seemed a little dicey, Amir had taken it because he was broke. So far, it had turned out ok, and his bosses seemed pleased with him. As long as he continued to draw the curious and turn a profit, the owners weren't about to question his abilities. After all, it took just as much skill to pull the wool over a customer's eyes as it did to look into those same bewildered pupils and divine the future.

Fortunately, he looked the part of a carnival psychic, which was half the battle in this business. With hair the color of spilled ink, a sallow complexion, a black Van Dyke beard, and a vibrant wardrobe of brightly colored shirts, scarves, and dungarees, Amir looked like he could have doubled as a stand-in for Zoltar in those fortune telling machines. He capped off the look with gold earrings in both ears, and a gaudy golden moon medallion which he wore around his neck at all times.

It was still early in the day, and there wouldn't be any fortune seekers for a while. Still, Amir thought it best to arrange the props in his wagon in case anyone got curious enough to weave their way through the flapping tents and seek out their destiny. Although it shouldn't have been such a source of confusion anymore, Amir simply couldn't understand how anyone could put their faith in crystals and runes and tea leaves and gypsy curses. Yet people lined up every night to throw their money at him and listen eagerly to the lies. He supposed that he shouldn't question the source of his livelihood, but sometimes, he found it difficult to keep leading these poor, mindless people around by the nose.

His guilt was definitely a character flaw for a swindler.

Once the crystal ball was polished, the incense was burning, and smoke was thick enough inside the cabin to hide the mirrors and camouflage the parlor tricks, Amir considered the old Magyar su-

49

perstitions of his grandmother and wondered for a moment if it was possible that he might have inherited her dubious gifts. She had been purported to divine fortunes from the entrails of ravens, making her living in much the same way Amir was doing with fraud and trickery in the side show. Of course, he had never believed the stories he heard about her and was equally doubtful of having adopted any of those telekinetic skills.

That was why it came as such a shock to him to hear someone whispering inside his wagon car when there was obviously no one there.

"I'll be here at midnight," the voice said. "I think you should be here too."

"Who's there," Amir asked, his eyes darting from corner to dimly-lit corner.

"Just Zeke," the voice replied. "Who did you think it was?"

Amir threw the door of his wagon open and listened for the sound of retreating footsteps. Save for the erratic pounding of sledgehammers and the groans of the men who wielded them, there was nothing to indicate than anybody was near his cabin. Amir circled the wagon, examining its underside carefully for any trace of a prankster. Surprisingly, there was nothing, not even the imprint of an athletic shoe in the dirt.

"I said I'll be here at midnight," Zeke reemphasized. "And there's a lot of money involved."

Not wanting to look foolish, Amir thoroughly searched every inch of the cabin for a portable radio that might have been broadcasting the dialogue as part of some old 1940's on-air crime drama. Of course, he didn't own anything like that. But that didn't mean someone else hadn't left one behind.

"Are you listening to me?" Zeke asked impatiently. "I've got $100,000 in a burlap sack and you can't even get excited enough to respond."

Although Amir couldn't see who was talking to him, he didn't automatically assume that it was someone from the other side of the void. That was more his grandmother's style. In fact, had his grandmother still been alive, she would have been chanting spells and activating curses on the wind to protect her from the mysterious voice. Amir couldn't bring himself to do that. Instead, he continued to search the cabin for any logical explanation and tried to remain calm at the prospect of $100,000.

"I'm taking my offer and leaving if you don't say something soon," Zeke said.

"I hear you, Zeke," he whispered at last. "Why don't you come out and show yourself?"

"It's not time for that yet. Worry instead about the rendezvous and the money."

"Fine," Amir conceded, feeling a little foolish talking to someone he couldn't even see. "I'll be here at midnight. Still, I would like to know what this is all about."

"There will be time for all that later," Zeke said. "It's better if you don't ask too many questions right now."

"Fine," Amir conceded.

"I knew you'd see it my way," Zeke replied. "Just make sure you bring a shovel tonight."

As the sun went down, and the moon seemed to blossom out of clouds and mist like a pale deadly flower, Amir paced back and forth in his cabin, wanting to call out to Zeke and discuss the matter further. But he felt foolish about doing such a thing, thinking that the whole scenario might have been a product of his imagination. It had certainly happened before to people who largely kept to themselves and lived alone. They grew lonely and subconsciously created personalities to keep them company, inventing fantasies to take them away from their humdrum lives. Maybe that's what Zeke was. Maybe that's what the promise of $100,000 at midnight was. Not knowing what else to do, Amir kept quiet and waited for the witching hour.

The brick that came through his window temporarily took his mind off his impatience.

"We don't lie to hard-working men and women, and neither should you," read the note that was tied to the brick. *"Just because your grandmother was good at this sort of thing doesn't mean you are."* It was signed, 'The Gang.'

It wasn't the first time something like this had happened, and it made Amir immediately suspicious of the midnight tryst that he had arranged with Zeke. It was no big secret among the other circus performers that he had no real abilities to speak of. There was also the fact that his fate didn't rest on his performance night after night, which only added to their irritation.

Understandably, some of those with actual skills—like the sword swallowers or the flame eaters—felt like their talents were trivialized by a lying gypsy. Until now, the jabs had always been good-natured, and Amir had taken them in fun. But the joke wasn't funny anymore, especially when the handwriting resembled Arnoldo the Acrobat's.

Normally, this was about the time every evening that Amir closed up shop and strolled over to the mess tent for a quick supper. But he didn't feel much like eating. He had just gone to the front door with the intent of securing the lock and spending a few hours in quiet contemplation, when he noticed a woman coming up the steps, anxious to hear what the future held.

The woman was dark-haired with eyes to match. She had a kind, trusting face, but her eyes were sad and downcast. Amir didn't need to be psychic to see that she had come here in hopes of learning some news that might give her hope. It was clear by the way she wrung her hands and forced herself to smile that life had dealt her a bum hand as of late. He didn't know what her problem was specifically, but it was clear she hoped he could help her.

Amir really wasn't in the mood to do any more pretending, but this was the only way he made his living. Besides, he knew it would take his mind off everything that had happened earlier on in the day. As it was, he didn't even get the chance to perpetrate his usual tricks and ruses.

"What can you tell me about my life?" the woman asked softly as she stepped into the trailer. "Will anything good ever happen to me?"

"Tell her she's got something of value in her purse," Zeke whispered.

"Would you mind emptying the contents of your bag onto the table," Amir asked, a little unnerved that the voice had returned. Arnoldo the Acrobat was probably laughing himself silly.

The hodgepodge of items from the handbag were typical of a woman: several tubes of lipstick, a compact, a loose assortment of change, a wallet, car keys and a hairbrush. For the life of him, Amir didn't know how any of these items could be valuable.

"That handful of change," Zeke nagged. "Look there."

Carefully, Amir rummaged through the gleaming money, noting for the first time that there was a particularly odd-looking coin amidst the normal quarters, dimes, and nickels.

"What is this?" he asked, holding the piece of gold up to the light.

"I found it on the street," the woman answered, leaning forward in her chair expectantly. "It probably came out of a gumball machine or something, but I thought it was kind of interesting."

"That coin dates all the way back to the Civil War and is worth more than three thousand dollars," Zeke said quietly.

Not daring to believe anything the voice told him for fear that it was actually another one of Arnoldo's tricks, Amir looked furtively around for any sign of a set-up. His trailer was a mishmash of gaudy trinkets, decor that looked like it might have been purchased at a carnival supply store, and all sorts of astrological paraphernalia. The walls of the trailer were covered in plush red velvet, and the floors were done in old cedar planks. The interior was decorated to look and feel old. It got close, but somehow still felt as artificial as Amir and his gift. As far as he could tell there was no possible place for anyone to hide, nor was there a spot to place a small microphone or any other electronic device.

"I'll tell you what," Amir said at last. "I think one of the sideshow barkers collects coins as a hobby. Why don't you go show this to him and see what he has to say about it? His name is John, and he has a long black handlebar mustache. You can't miss him."

The woman nodded agreeably and rushed out the door with the coin clutched tightly in her hand.

A half hour later she returned, her face aglow like one of the fire breather's torches. "He said I could get a couple of thousand for this. at least," she gushed, plunking a small wad of money down on the table for Amir's fee. "Apparently, this is quite the find. I never in a million years would have guessed that this would be worth so much."

That was exactly what Amir was afraid of. Arnoldo was quite the practical joker. But he wasn't that good. Not nearly that good. Besides, it was unlikely that he had gone to this length to perpetrate a lie. Like the other nightly performers in the Carnival of Chaos, Arnoldo had his act and his life to worry about. He simply wouldn't have time to plot something this elaborate.

"It fell out of a collector's briefcase," Zeke

whispered. "But you don't have to throw that part in. She would only want to return it. She's the honest type."

Although it was a bit hypocritical, Amir was a little disturbed by the fact that Zeke didn't pride himself on his honesty. However, he tried to push that minor sticking point aside as he imagined himself with his share of a hundred thousand dollars. The possibility of wealth seemed more realistic now that he was fairly certain Arnoldo and Zeke weren't the same person. That didn't mean he was comfortable with the whole thing. Still, it made him feel a little better. With that kind of money, he could leave this freaky circus behind. He didn't know how he would break the news to The Shadow Brothers. But he would worry about that problem later.

Amir waited until the crowds started thinning before he slipped out under the cover of moonlight and headed to the supply truck for a shovel. When he returned to his cabin at two minutes to midnight, he wasn't at all sure what to expect. The small wagon was exactly as he had left it, dimly lit and scarcely haunted.

"Are you there?" he called out. "It's me, Amir."

"I'm here," Zeke replied.

"You can come out now," Amir said. "I'm alone."

"I'm standing right beside you," Zeke replied, obviously enjoying himself. Amir made a complete circle, diligently searching for the man he knew wasn't really there.

"You're a ghost," Amir said, hardly believing the words were coming from his mouth.

"For now," Zeke answered, as though it was inconsequential. "Did you bring what I told you to?"

"I've got the shovel."

"Good. Now walk where I tell you to."

Amir did as he was told, taking a few paces forward, a few more to the right, and then following Zeke's voice as it directed him by means of 'hot' and 'cold'. Instead of going toward the main tent and the heart of the dwindling circus, Zeke led him away from the nexus of excitement. Even at this late hour, Amir could still hear the strongman and a couple of the magicians playing poker by lantern light. He stepped softly, hoping to make as little noise as he could. Fortunately, he didn't have to go very far before Zeke told him to stop walking and start digging.

Even as he transplanted the first shovelful of dirt, Amir had a number of unanswered questions that made him uneasy the more he thought about them.

"Why me?" Amir huffed as he pitched dirt in the moonlight. "Out of all the people you could have whispered to, why did you choose me?"

"It's in your blood," Zeke said. "Not everybody can hear the voices of the dead. But you can. Your heritage is chock full of listeners. It's embedded in your genetics like blonde hair or blue eyes. It echoes through the generations."

Amir immediately thought of his grandmother and wondered if she had really been as crazy as everybody thought she was. For the first time, he considered the distinct possibility that there might have actually been something to all that gypsy mumbo-jumbo. It scared him more than a little to think that he might have inherited that dubious gift.

"So, you're telling me that there hasn't been anyone else pass through here that was capable of hearing you?"

"Think about this," Zeke said impatiently. "The Carnival of Chaos sets up in this abandoned field on the outskirts of town. Nothing grows here. There's no decent supply of animals to attract wild game hunters. It's too rocky for kids to play baseball. And it's too exposed for camping. There is absolutely no reason why anyone would step foot on this field. It could have easily been another twenty years before anybody got within earshot. It could have been another fifty years before anybody with the ability to hear me actually wandered close enough. I guess this was simply good luck. Well, that and your gypsy blood."

Temporarily satisfied, Amir dug his shovel deep into the ground.

"You're getting closer," Zeke whispered gently as Amir stabbed at the earth. He was out of breath and sweating long before he had gone more than a couple of feet deep. Then he struck something that didn't give like the soft dirt had. It was a relief from the monotonous, backbreaking work, but it immediately made him wary of what he might find. Long before he cleared the thin layer of dust away, Amir knew that it was a bag of some sort. The only question in his mind was whether it contained a hundred thousand dollars in unmarked bills or something more sinister.

"Thatta boy," Zeke encouraged him as Amir knelt down and heaved the sack out of the freshly dug hole.

Cinched with a length of hemp rope, the bag seemed unusually heavy. Eager to see what was inside yet wary of what he might find, Amir carefully undid the knot and dumped the contents on the damp ground. The skull stared at him balefully with moonlit eyes, the zenith on a mountain of bones. Although it was dark outside, there was still enough illumination to see the large crack that spread outward in spider-webbing patterns from a nasty looking break in the skull.

"Is this you?" Amir asked.

"What's left of me."

"There's no money here," Amir said. "You lied."

"Not at all. This is the first step to finding the money. My partner and I knocked over an armored car, and then he hit me with the shovel that we used to bury the money. He dumped me in a shallow grave, just far enough down to be concealed, yet close enough to the elements to speed the decaying process."

"That explains the hole in your head," Amir noted, picking up the skull and glancing at the wound with equal parts fascination and revulsion. "But I'm still a little confused. What good is a hundred dollars to a restless spirit?"

"The money is irrelevant to me," Zeke said. "But it's not to my partner. After what he did to me with the business end of that shovel, I want to make sure he doesn't get anything for his trouble."

"So how do you know he hasn't already gone back for the cash?"

"As you can see, my partner didn't bury me with the money. Still, a little of me was left on that burlap sack, a few drops of blood that I can still feel.

61

Because of that, I know exactly where the money is. And for some strange reason, it hasn't moved, even though it's been years since the heist. But I know Murray. He'll go back for it eventually. I just want him to be surprised when the hole he digs turns up nothing more than a few earthworms."

Amir thought about this for a moment, feeling as though something didn't seem right. He held the skull up and looked deep into those empty sockets, unsure of what he hoped to find. "You want to be the one to get the money?" he repeated, not at all sure what that meant. "You're dead. A heap of bones. How are you going to go back for the money?"

Yet, in a flash of moonlight, Amir knew exactly how the spirit planned to do it. Vertigo gripped him as he fell out of his body, much like the feeling you get late at night when it seems like you're about to tumble off the bed only to find that you're lying a good foot and a half away from the edge.

Picking the skull up had been his mistake, and it now, it seemed, he would pay for eternity. Zeke had stolen his body for his own nefarious purposes, leaving Amir to inhabit the heap of decaying bones he had left behind.

"I never promised you any money," Zeke said, using what had once been Amir's mouth. "I just said that there was a lot of money involved, and you assumed that I was giving you a chance at it."

Amir realized it all too well, only it was too late to do anything other than stare sightlessly up through empty sockets of bone that had seen too much murder and thievery in their time.

"Sorry to do this to you," Zeke said apologetically. "But business is business, and I've got some that's still unfinished. Old Murray will never guess that it's me, wearing your skin and bones. Yet I suppose that's the beauty of it. He'll never realize what hit him until it's too late. I'll be sure to look him in the eyes though before he closes them for the last time. I want him to see who it really was that buried that hatchet in his back or split his skull with a sledgehammer. I want him to see that death didn't stop me, and that I'm taking what's mine."

Up until this point, Amir had been totally dissatisfied with his life, feeling that he should have made something more out of himself than a hustling fraud who earned his living off other people's gullibility. Now, the life that had been stolen from him by the greedy spirit meant more to him than anything else. Yet, it was too late to do anything. Instead, Amir could only watch through a corpse's eyes as the man that used to be him ran off into the night.

Amir hated Zeke for what he had done, and unable to do anything else, thought about how foolish he had been. Still, he wondered if there wasn't some way out of this mess. Obviously, he was special, made so by the Magyar blood in his veins. Surely there was some advantage in that.

Amir suddenly felt a thrill of excitement as an idea occurred to him, and had he still been in possession of his body, the chill that ran through his essence would have probably manifested itself as a smile.

***

It would have killed Arnoldo the Acrobat's soul to know that he had something in common with Amir.

He heard his name being called like a song in the night. Curious, he slipped quietly out of his trailer and followed the voice. It frightened him a little to hear his name chanted over and over in the darkness like a black litany, but it puzzled him too. When he stumbled upon the pile of bones, he nearly cried out in terror, but stopped himself just shy of a scream.

The dread ended a few moments later as Amir walked away from those dismal bones looking as though he were capable of walking a tightrope or swinging from a trapeze. He only wondered if Zeke would recognize him in the body of an acrobat.

Although it was well past midnight, and the

Carnival of Chaos was officially closed, a few side-shows were still open, promising the bizarre and uncanny in exchange for a few tokens. As a general rule of thumb, the sideshow freaks would perform until the money stopped changing hands. In places starved for entertainment, this sometimes went on until the wee hours of the morning, and Amir was hopeful that Zeke was still here somewhere, looking for his old partner and the lost money.

Amir only had to take a few steps down swindler's alley before he saw the man he had formerly been, except without any of the heart and soul. It was Zeke, wearing his body like a badly-tailored suit and eyeing a scruffy-looking man with a bad eye, and tattoos that ran the length of his forearms. The man was throwing a softball at three empty milk cans, trying to win a teddy bear for his girlfriend. It was Eugene's booth, and Amir knew it well. He had suffered more than a little humiliation when walking past that particular section of the midway.

"Arnoldo," Eugene said amiably. "How are things on the high wire?"

"Well, I didn't fall tonight, and I guess that's a good thing," Amir said, trying to respond as Arnoldo might have. Eugene nodded agreeably, trading Murray another softball for his dollar.

"I'm going to win one of these stuffed gorillas

for you, babe," Murray said to his girlfriend. "It's just taking me a little longer than I thought."

"Excuse me," Zeke said, tapping Murray's girlfriend on the shoulder. "When your boyfriend gets finished playing, stop by my wagon and I'll give you a free tarot reading. I can predict the future, you know? Of course, if you had come to me first, I could have told you how many tries it would take to win that gorilla."

Without the slightest hesitation, Eugene reached underneath the counter and pulled out a Louisville Slugger.

"Go cheat somebody else, you foreign fraud," he shouted at the man that looked and spoke like Amir. "These are my customers. Go find some of your own."

"I was just trying to be friendly," Zeke said. "These two look like they have a particularly bright future ahead, and I just thought they might like to have a glance at what the coming months might hold."

"How would you like a look at what I might hold?" Eugene said, picking up the baseball bat for emphasis.

"Let's try once more, babe," Murray said, obviously nervous at the prospect of trouble. "Then if you want, we'll see what's in the cards for us."

Eugene set the baseball bat across the counter

to reemphasize his threat. He turned his attention back to the man he thought was Arnoldo.

"You don't look so good, Arnoldo. Everything OK?"

"Just an upset stomach," Amir said, as he watched Zeke lead the unsuspecting couple back to the wagon. "You know how this circus food wreaks havoc on the old digestive tract."

"I think it's probably the phony gypsy-boy that's making you sick," Eugene said loudly enough for Murray and his girlfriend to hear as they walked away. "Anybody that can't earn an honest living certainly turns my stomach."

"It's the food," Amir insisted.

"Maybe you should lie down or something then," Eugene suggested. "Take a Pepcid. Relax. Stop doing flips and somersaults for a while."

"Maybe I should," Amir agreed as he quickly left to follow Zeke and Murray.

He arrived at the wagon just in time to watch Zeke stare deep into Murray's eyes and smile. He peeped in through the broken window, glad that he hadn't taken any initiative to fix it after that brick came through it.

"Guess who, old buddy?" Zeke said. "It's been a long time since we knocked over that Wells Fargo truck."

Murray recoiled from Zeke as if from a venomous snake.

"You haven't gone back for the money yet, have you?" Zeke asked.

Murray's mouth worked to form words that wouldn't come out. "I don't know anything about any money."

"Don't play stupid with me. This is your partner you're talking to here, not a stranger."

"I've never seen you before," Murray said nervously.

"Honey, who is this?" Murray's girlfriend asked impatiently.

"I don't know," Murray admitted. "I've never laid eyes on this guy."

"Not in this body, of course. But you remember old Zeke. I'm sure of that. You remember going to The Black Cat before we knocked over that truck, and watching those girls dance. You remember hitting that armored car, stealing the money, hitting me in the back of the head with a shovel. You remember all of it, I'm sure."

Murray looked scared and alone.

"Do you remember, Murray?"

Murray nodded his head slowly.

"Why didn't you go back for the money? What happened to keep you from profiting from my murder?"

"What money?" Murray's girlfriend asked, whining a little now. "Did you really kill somebody?"

"Shut up, Lucille. We'll talk about this later."

Lucille looked like she had been slapped. But she didn't say anything else.

"I've been in jail," Murray said with a sigh. "The closed-circuit camera in the back of that armored car got our faces on tape. They eventually caught up with me. Nobody ever found what was left of you. I did ten years in the clink for that money. I've been out a couple of months now."

"We hit the truck across the state line. I'm surprised they tracked you down."

"Well, they did. Our pictures were posted in lots of places with high visibility. Lots of people had a look at our mugs, and one of them eventually pointed the finger."

"But you're out now, and you still haven't gone after the cash."

"They're still watching me, expecting me to lead them straight to the stash. That's why I've waited. I wanted to let things calm down a bit."

"You didn't want to lead them to the money, and yet you've come back to the very town that we hid it in?"

"I grew up in Valley Falls," Murray said. "I've

never lived anywhere else. If I went someplace different, that's when people would start to wonder. That's when the questions would start flying and the police would be watching me 24-7. I thought it would be best to act normal, let some of the attention die down. Then, when everyone forgot about me, I would dig up the bag. I don't guess I'll get that chance now."

"What is everyone talking about?" Murray's girlfriend shouted insistently.

Zeke seemed more than happy to reply, pulling out a knife that Amir sometimes used as a prop during seances that required blood. "Oh, nothing but a little armed robbery between friends," Zeke said, obviously enjoying himself. "Right, Murray?"

"You're dead," Murray kept muttering over and over, spittle forming at the edges of his mouth like a rabid dog. "You're dead. I killed you, and you are dead. That's not even what you looked like, and yet it's you. But you're dead."

"I think you've got it backwards," Zeke said as he slammed the knife into Murray's stomach. "You're the one who's dead."

Murray's girlfriend screamed once and loudly. Zeke ripped the knife out of his partner's gut and lunged at Lucille, slitting her throat in one fluid motion. The screaming sounded like it was coming from the bottom of a clogged drain, gurgling and watery. Then everything went silent save for the faint, unmistakable sound of a calliope in one of the ill-lit tents. Amir gasped as he watched the blood trickle across the wagon's floorboards, dripping through the gaps and splashing onto the dusty ground. He managed to hide just before Zeke came out carrying a shovel and smiling with teeth that weren't his own.

Amir followed him and smiled a similarly alien smile as he got an idea.

Zeke went up to the edge of one of the clown's trailers, sniffed the air for familiar blood, and began to dig. Amir waited until all the shovel work had been done and the burlap sack was pulled out of the ground before daring to creep closer. Zeke was too enraptured by the prospect of easy living to hear anyone approaching. It was only as Zeke was thumbing through the stacks upon stacks of bills that Amir quietly grabbed the shovel.

"A hundred thou," Zeke said. "Eat your heart out, Murray."

"It's a little past midnight, I know," Amir said, startling Zeke. "But I made it after all. I guess this sort of throws a monkey wrench in the plans, huh? Should we divvy up the take now or wait a while and discuss it over a couple of beers?"

Zeke whirled around, the glee temporarily gone from the eyes he had stolen. He was confused by the acrobat that stood in front of him. "Who are you? You were the guy at the test-your-luck booth."

"Oh, I'm much more than that. But a smart guy like you shouldn't have any problem figuring that out," Amir said just before he swung the shovel. It pained him a little to see his old body in such a bloody state of disrepair, but not so much so that he neglected the money that lay on the ground in myriad, red-spattered piles.

It was quite a bit of work digging the grave, but Amir did it quickly and without thought. No job had ever paid as well as this one, and he knew that his life would take a turn for the better once the last shovelful of dirt was replaced. So, he dug as though the keys to his life were in China. His old body made a thud as it hit bottom, and Amir wasted no time transplanting the soil he had broken loose. But he stopped just before covering up what was left of the face he had once worn.

"All that work, Zeke, and here's what you've got to show for it," he said, thinking out loud. "Then again, maybe not."

Amir peeled a twenty-dollar bill off the top of one of the bundles of cash and threw it nonchalantly onto the upturned face that he had only vague remembrances of now. And then he started shoveling again. "That was a down payment on my new life," Amir said, thankful that he wouldn't have to swindle or lie or cheat honest, hardworking people anymore.

Of course, he knew it would only be a matter of time before Zeke whispered to some other poor, unsuspecting soul and persuaded them to dig him up. Amir could only speculate on what sort of face Zeke would wear the next time he came back for the money. Amir thought with a smile that he wouldn't have to worry about such a confrontation. After all, he had a hundred thousand dollars at his disposal, and faces could easily be changed even if stony hearts remained the same.

Yet, he wasn't so sure that Zeke was going to be his main problem. There, framed in moonlight, was one of the magicians hanging from the overhanging branch of a tree by the bends of his legs. It reminded Amir of a gymnast dangling from the trapeze. Yet as far as Amir knew, the magician didn't possess any athletic skills to speak of. Still, he swung back and forth like a pendulum, like a practiced acrobat.

"I think you've got something that belongs to me," the magician said.

Amir thought he was talking about the money

at first. But then he realized whose body he inhabited and knew that it wasn't the magician looking out through those eyes.

"I want my body back," Arnoldo said.

Amir watched as the magician dropped from the tree and came at him. The shovel worked as well the second time as it did the first. Arnoldo went down immediately.

This time, however, Amir wasn't going to take any chances. Hacking the body up into pieces with blades from the sword swallower's tent was tough work, but Amir made himself go through with the bloody mess. Then he scattered the remains, hopefully making it impossible for Arnoldo to come after him.

He didn't really understand how this whole body-swapping business worked. But he was fairly sure that Arnoldo wouldn't be back. Knowing that he wouldn't rest well until he completed the messy business, Amir dug up what was left of Zeke and diced him up like a summer onion. As he hid the last severed limb in a burned-out tree, he sighed with the realization that he would never hear his name whispered again in the still moonlight.

Still, something didn't feel right. He made it to the edge of the carnival grounds before he heard the preternatural scream of panthers in their cells, and grizzly bears growling in their padlocked habitats. Amir had often heard from the trainers that animals instinctively knew when something was wrong. After all that had happened, Amir wasn't surprised to hear them tonight.

What he was surprised to hear was the crash of breaking glass, and several men screaming. The screams were short lived. Then there was only the faint hush of a breeze and the rustling of grass in the distance.

Although he had nothing concrete to base his fear on, Amir ran for his life.

He shivered at the thought that he might have been wrong about the way souls jumped from host to host. Maybe it wasn't necessary that they be human. Maybe it didn't matter if the discarded body was all in one piece. Unwilling to look back over his shoulder, Amir could hear something big moving through the brush behind him. He kept his eyes focused on the trail ahead and the road that lay past it. The last thing he wanted to see was a fierce predator like a panther or a grizzly with revenge on its mind. That's why he didn't turn around.

He wasn't sure if Zeke or Arnoldo was after him, and it really didn't matter. What mattered is that he would never be able to truly relax now for fear that someone or something was sneaking up behind him, bent on revenge, and riding an unfamiliar body like a jockey. Amir would have gladly given up all the money in the burlap sack just to be rid of the threat. But he didn't think it worked that way. Whatever was chasing him didn't seem to think so either. It was frightening to consider what Arnoldo or Zeke might be capable of in a panther's body.

Amir reached the blacktop road seconds before a beat-up Ford topped the hill. Fortunately, the old man behind the wheel stopped for Amir when he held out his thumb.

Amir felt better about things as the old truck rumbled down the road, leaving the threat behind him. Then the old man smiled, showing tobacco-blackened teeth and an unsettling sparkle in his eye. It probably meant nothing. Then again...

Amir knew he would never trust another face again. Not even the one he saw in the mirror.

HOLE IN THE SKY

Walter moved his knight into position with a strong, liver-spotted hand. Smiling and obviously satisfied with himself, he snatched up the opposing queen and placed it alongside the chess board with the rest of Jack's beaten army.

Jack scowled at him, but there was no real malice behind the look. He had learned to accept defeat over the years.

"You never learn, preacher," Walter said, laughing to himself. "I've beat you a hundred times at chess, and I'll probably beat you a hundred more. I actually think you're getting worse at this game."

"I hate chess," Jack replied, backing away from the table.

"Come on," Walter laughed. "Don't leave so soon. I want to finish slaughtering you."

"Senile old fool," Jack mumbled under his breath. "Just because he was a Marine he always thinks he's supposed to win."

"Sit back down," Walter said pleadingly. "Just for a few more minutes. The misery shouldn't last long."

Jack hesitated for a moment and then begrudgingly sat back down in the lawn chair. But it wasn't because he had any real desire to finish the game or to prolong Walter's winning streak. The truth of the matter was, his joints were achy, and he didn't really feel like walking the distance to the main house. If he had even mentioned wanting to go in and lie down, Walter would have probably made some sort of sarcastic remark about Jack being incontinent or needing Viagra or having a fiber deficiency, and Jack was in no mood for wit or sarcasm.

Walter, at times, had a tendency to ramble on about his indestructible chess game or his glory days as a footsoldier or his ongoing affair with the blonde nurse in west wing or any number of other things that he was better at than Jack. But only when you got him going. And Jack had no intention of doing that. So, he sat back down to the chess game and tried his best to lose quickly.

"You're ruthless, you know that?" Jack said through clenched teeth, wanting desperately to be elsewhere.

"Absolutely," Walter replied. "And you're not ruthless enough. I guess all those years behind the pulpit dulled your wit."

"Meaning what?"

"Meaning you had no reason to think for yourself when you had God thinking for you."

"The same could be said for you," Jack said defensively, positioning his rook. "I don't imagine there were a lot of open-minded grunts back in your day. 'Yes sir' and 'no sir' doesn't exactly strike me as innovative thinking."

"I wasn't always a grunt," Walter said, growing a little perturbed.

"And I wasn't always a minister," Jack replied.

"Thank God for some things," Walter replied sarcastically, a disgusted look smeared across his face like a disease.

"Like you would know anything about thanking God," Jack was quick to add.

Temporarily beaten, Walter studied the chess board to avoid glowering at Jack.

Jack, meanwhile, sat there patiently, watching his friend as he fumed and plotted his next move. It was sort of funny, he thought to himself, how seriously Walter took all of this. Everything was always some sort of contest to him, and naturally he was supposed to be the winner. But he had been like that for as long as Jack had known him, always striving to be better than everyone else, loathing defeat, feeling like everything he did was of prodigious importance. Jack supposed they were admirable qualities, although they did grow annoying at times like these when he was ready to stretch out on his bed and take a nap.

Jack wasn't even sure why they still bothered to play chess anymore. He never won, never even came close for that matter. But it was to be expected. After all, Walter was a retired Marine officer. Warfare strategy and field positioning were old hat to him. Jack, on the other hand, was more accustomed to battling for souls instead of the bodies that held them. It was something Walter had never understood, no matter how many times Jack tried to explain it.

"I guess today you're fighting for the lost, and I'm fighting for blood, just like always," Walter said with a smirk as he studied the board.

"We've already had this discussion before," Jack said tiredly.

"Has anyone ever seen a soul?" Walter asked sarcastically. "Does anyone know what one looks like?"

"Has anyone ever seen the wind?" Jack responded quickly.

"No," Walter answered smartly, "but they've seen the effects of the wind. And I've never seen the effect of a soul."

"Still, they're worth fighting for."

"Jack, you can fight for souls all you want, but it's a losing battle. Me, I'd rather fight for my country, my countrymen, freedom, vengeance. Things that I can see or feel. And since I'm too old to do that now, I suppose I'll just play chess to show you that I'm better than you. Beliefs included."

Jack looked at Walter as if he had a third eye in the center of his forehead.

"Every time we've played, I've beat you," Walter insisted. "That has to count for something."

"Only that you're better at chess than me. Not that you're right about everything."

"That remains to be seen," Walter replied.

"Are you going to move sometime in this century?" Jack asked him at last. "The next millennium will be here any minute now."

"Keep your shorts on, Moses. Greatness takes time, you know. Do you think Napoleon or Alexander the Great made many decisions off the cuff?"

"Fine. Take your time, Genghis." Jack said with a sigh, tilting his head back to stare at the clouds. On occasion, when Walter was busy planning the War of 1812 or reenacting Waterloo in his mind, Jack would look up at the sky and try to spot familiar people in the layers of cirrus and cumulonimbus.

Today, however, there were no faces or clouds. Instead, there was a fiery hole in the sky like a bleeding wound in heaven that made Jack gasp for breath and fall out of his lawn chair.

Walter immediately sprang up from his seat. "Jack?" he said. "You ok?"

"I'm fine," Jack said, keeping his eyes focused on the heavens. Walter offered Jack his hand and helped him back to his feet.

"What is it?" Walter asked, looking up to see what his friend was watching.

"Go get your binoculars," Jack ordered. "The ones you look through when the nurses are undressing."

"Anything else I can get for you while I'm gone?" Walter said sarcastically to show that he wasn't used to taking orders. "A Perrier? Sunscreen? A magazine?"

Jack scowled at his friend. "Just go," he said.

Eventually, Walter returned with a set of field glasses that he had used during his days in the service. Jack snatched them from him without a word and pointed them at the flaming sky. His hands trembled as his eyes scanned the heavens for the first signs of war.

"Well, what is it?" Walter asked him, clueless.

"Angels," he said simply, as if it was the most

commonplace of occurrences.

"Are you senile?"

"Look for yourself," Jack responded, handing over the binoculars.

Walter looked up but didn't seem too surprised by what he saw.

"Those are angels, aren't they, Jack?" Walter asked calmly, staring a hole through the chess board.

"Yes," Jack said, sighing, "I would say so. And judging by the weapons and war chariots, they're getting ready to fight again."

A look of confusion crossed Walter's face like a shadow. "Again, you said? This has happened before?" At last, a battle he hadn't heard about or studied or reenacted with his tiny plastic soldiers, and his bulletin boards spattered with red flags and push pins.

Jack nodded.

"When?"

"In a vision given to John the Apostle on the island of Patmos, where he was being held as a prisoner."

"You mean in the Bible?"

"Yes," answered Jack, "The Book of Revelation." He paused to remember the passage. "And there was war in heaven. Michael and his angels fought against the dragon, and the dragon fought and his angels, and prevailed not; neither was their place found any more in heaven."

"What are you talking about?"

"And the great dragon was cast out," continued Jack, "that old serpent, called the Devil, and Satan, which deceiveth the whole world: he was cast out into earth and his angels were cast out with him."

Walter chewed on this for a minute, his brow knitting in confusion.

Although he knew it was wrong to feel this way, Jack couldn't help but feel a small sense of satisfaction after witnessing Walter's response. He had tried on numerous occasions to lead his friend to the faith only to be vehemently turned away and scoffed at. "Nonsense," Walter would always say, laughing at Jack and his religion. Now, however, he needed a healthy dose of salt and pepper to make those words edible. And Jack was ready to watch him eat.

Soon, however, the mists of tears and blood that fell from heaven made it easy to forget about Walter. Amazed and reluctant to be a part of such a grisly baptism, Jack turned his eyes toward the skies and watched grimly as archangels amassed their troops for war. Battalions of winged soldiers flew in formation, carrying savage weapons. The clouds looked awash with the blood of angels perhaps, or saints, and it was all Jack could do not to scream. But he knew that Walter was watching his every move, so he tried to remain calm. If faith meant losing control when everything started to fall apart, then Walter would never want to know God. And Jack knew how much Walter valued strength, so he stood like a statue with his eyes turned toward Heaven.

"Aren't you going to finish this game?" Walter asked Jack, trying to evade the obvious topics of conversation.

Jack gave his friend a cursory glance, knowing that the man was frightened but afraid to show it. Yet in that brief glimpse, he saw more hatred than fear, and he wondered just what it was that was burning deep inside Walter.

"Well?" Walter persisted.

"Are you blind?" Jack asked, dumbfounded and confused. "I think what's going on up there is a little more important than some stupid game."

Walter didn't say anything at first. He simply nodded his head in what could have been construed as agreement. Then, he studied the chess board for another moment, and grimacing, wiped it clean of what few pieces remained.

For the moment, Walter was more intriguing than the battalions of rebellious angels. In all the years he had known his friend, Jack had never known

Walter to give in when he was winning. And yet, here he was throwing away a perfectly good victory.

Jack could tell by the way Walter was grimacing and keeping his eyes focused on the blank chess board that he was reeling inside. Yet, Jack couldn't help but believe that all those years of sweating bullets and dodging them should have hardened Walter to the concept of death. Still, the sweat was pouring off the man's brow.

"Jack," he said as he rearranged the chess pieces. "Do you ever feel like you're being pulled in a direction that you don't want to go?"

Jack took his eyes away from the binoculars for a moment and focused them on his friend. Maybe Walter was about to come to his senses and accept everything Jack had tried to tell him over the past few years. Maybe the tug of God was just too strong.

"Lots of times," Jack replied, hoping he would say the right things. "Especially when I was being called into the ministry."

"Then answer something for me."

"OK. What is it you want to know?"

"If God is a perfect being, how does He create things that aren't?"

"It would have to be one of those kinds of questions," Jack said reluctantly, sensing that Walter might actually be scared enough to listen for a change.

"And what kind is that?" Walter asked, a little offended.

"Unanswerable. Like the question, 'If God is all powerful, could He conceivably create a rock so big that even He couldn't move it?'"

"In other words, you don't know."

"Does anyone? Maybe evil is allowed to thrive in order to show how powerful God is. The angels start to think that they're a little high and mighty. Then they become prideful and sin. Then He crushes them and throws them out of Heaven. There. An instant display of authority."

"Or maybe," Walter interjected with a little more strength in his voice, "He just can't stop it."

Jack tore his attentions away from heaven and studied his pitiful friend for a moment. Walter didn't seem to notice Jack. He had already started setting up the chess board again in a different configuration. Obviously, he had made up his mind on the matter.

And Jack, like usual, felt like he had said the wrong thing. "What are you doing?" Jack asked, hoping for some answers.

"I'm plotting," he replied cryptically.

"Plotting?"

"Yes. Keeping track of the war. Those pieces on your side are God's and these over here, the ones on my side, are the rebel angels. I would have let you lead the revolt on Heaven, but I thought I might be better suited to it."

Jack frowned, pitying his friend for his ignorance. No matter how hard he tried, he just couldn't understand how Walter could miss the obvious truth, written across the sky in fire and blood. But maybe, he thought, Walter hadn't missed the truth so much as avoided it. Or been led to avoid it.

As Walter was busy arranging the knights and pawns and bishops into some semblance of the conflict above, Jack noticed something that he had always known was there. Tattooed across the back of the colonel's right hand were the words, 'Die Young,' in prison-blue ink, looking more like a cattle brand now than any attempt at toughness or military fashion. Walter had explained all about getting the tattoo during the war when he thought that getting shipped home in a body bag was the most likely outcome. But now, something else came to mind, as Jack studied the heavens, watching demons forge their flaming swords with lightning and hellfire.

"You know, Jack," Walter said, not bothering to hide the venom in his voice. "Strategy is essential to winning a war. Without the right commander in charge of things, you may as well hand over your country and wave the white flag. That may have been why God didn't have any reason to be afraid during that first revolt. The Devil was a poor tactician. But then again, he hadn't served in the Marines."

Jack heard the words but didn't really take the time to analyze them. He was too busy watching Walter's liver-spotted hand plot and plan the great war, the words 'Die Young' proclaiming a lie each time they moved in front of Jack's eyes.

"And the beast causeth all, both small and great, rich and poor, free and bond, to receive a mark in their right hand, or in their foreheads," he mumbled.

"What was that?" Walter asked.

"Oh, nothing. I was just talking to myself," Jack answered, thinking all the while that Walter might have sold his soul long ago so that he might outlive the tattoo on his hand. This second wave of rebel angels was sure to need an experienced tactician planning their moves for them. Who was to say that Walter hadn't struck some sort of deal with them in the earliest stages of their revolt? This deal might have been made in some sweltering jungle when Walter was sure he was going to die. Or it might never have been made at all.

Overhead, the clouds were starting to darken and swell as if recently bruised. The fiery hole in the sky had gone from a blazing orange to a deep red. It looked like it could rain blood at any moment now.

"You know," Walter said with a devilish smile, "it would be a funny thing if we could actually control the angels up there by simply maneuvering our chess pieces down here."

"Yeah, hysterical. A celestial war game played by a couple of over-the-hill windbags who have little else to do with their time but sit around a chess board. Who in their right mind would trust the fate of the universe to us and our game?"

"Oh, I don't know," Walter smirked, moving one of his black knights.

Lightning tore the sky apart like a set of strong hands. Strangely, there was no rain to follow it. Only thunder, like the sound of war drums, and the streaks of electricity which set Heaven on fire.

Jack backed away from the table, suddenly fearful of Walter and whatever he might be capable of.

"Well," Walter asked impatiently from across the battlefield, "are you going to play or let all of Heaven be destroyed?"

Jack couldn't believe what he had heard. He was suddenly sure of his senility. "Walter, have you lost your marbles? Or worse, have I?"

"What do you mean?"

"Do you...think we're crazy?"

"Of course I do," Walter was quick to respond.

"You've got to be a little off your rocker to cope with the world these days. The world's a crazy place to live in. Insanity just makes it easier to survive. It helps you fit in."

Jack thought about this for a moment. He slid a rook in front of his king for protection. Thunder shook the table with holy hands, rattling the pieces on the board. Jack looked at his hand in awe, as if lightning might leap from the tips of his fingers.

"Just remember, Jack. You've never beat me at this game. Heaven doesn't stand a chance."

Jack really didn't believe that he had rallied angels around the Almighty. Instead, he chalked the whole thing up to senility and fatigue. Everything, that was, except for the rain which began, first in a mist and then a steady drizzle, christening one with water from Heaven and drowning the other in the blood of martyred men. Only, for the life of him, Jack couldn't figure out which one of them was gasping for breath beneath the surface.

Walter, however, seemed to be breathing just fine.

"That's quite a light show up there, isn't it?" he asked Jack, smirking like a fool.

Jack looked up and saw the sky was filled with falling stars, burning to ash before they touched the earth. He snatched the field glasses from Walter and watched the angels cry and wail as they crashed down from Heaven. Their feathers were bloody, their wings torn like flies' wings, and their eyes were focused on the eternal city for one last look.

Walter shifted a bishop and removed Jack's knight. Jack tore his hearing aid from his ear as angels cried out in torment and sadness.

"What are you doing?" Jack asked, his eyes darting from Walter to the rain of angels and back to Walter.

"I'm playing chess," Walter answered calmly.

Jack gritted his false teeth and tentatively advanced a pawn, hoping that it was the right move.

Walter started to laugh.

"Jack," he said in between laughs, "you are definitely getting worse at this."

Jack closed his eyes and prayed to God, as Walter made his next move and the blood of saints began to patter down on their bald heads and cardigan-covered shoulders. Suddenly, Jack wished for senility. It would be so much easier knowing that he didn't really know anything at all, that everything was just a daydream his tired, incoherent brain had spit out in a fit of mental vomiting.

But the fact of the matter was he did know some things. Foremost among them was that he would never be able to beat Walter at chess. It was pointless to even think along those lines. Despairing, Jack looked to the skies, to the gaping wound in the clouds, and felt his hope drain away like blood from a cut. He felt a little like Atlas, sitting there in his chair, eyes focused on Heaven, knowing all the while that his knowledge of some silly little medieval game would decide the fate of mankind. The weight of the world was on his shoulders, and he felt like his brittle spine might give way at any moment.

Walter smiled at him from across the table, his hair matted to his head, wet with sweat and blood.

Jack shivered and began to pray silently. Replacing his hearing aid, he moved another piece hoping to hear the screaming and howling of the rebel angels as they were thrown out of the holy city. All he heard instead was the clash of metal, and the dull thud of bodies crashing to the earth. Jack thought of screaming for them as they fell silently, but his voice was too weak.

His hands, however, felt fine. Although it didn't really make sense to attack someone who was an ex-Marine, Jack also knew that it was just as foolish to sit there idly twiddling his thumbs while the man across from him made martyrs out of the angelic hosts. Walter was taken by surprise as Jack grabbed him by the throat and squeezed until the flow of air into his lungs was cut off. The old Marine struggled beneath the minister's weight, tried to bring his hands up to defend himself, looked to Heaven for help when there was none coming.

And still, Jack tightened his grip. Jack, of course, knew that it was a sin to murder. But he also knew that God would forgive him.

Walter, on the other hand, wasn't nearly as agreeable. The Marine glared at Jack with hatred, his eyes bulging in their sockets like hard-boiled eggs.

Jack called to God for strength and squeezed until he felt Walter go limp in his arms. Only once, as he was wiping the spattering of blood off of his face, did Jack even wonder about his senility.

With the deed done, and the flies gathering in swarms, Jack left Walter where he was and stood on shaky legs. He could feel his hands trembling, sticky from dried blood, so totally unlike the hands he had known. It was almost as if he had become someone else in the past few minutes.

Although he wasn't entirely sure of what was happening to him, he wiped the chess board clean of Walter's army. Somewhere in Heaven a trumpet sounded a victory note, and the lightning immediately stopped. Jack looked up in time to see the slain rebel angels plummeting to earth and then through the earth to somewhere much worse. Their feathers fell in bloody clumps.

"Why does God choose to let evil persist?" Jack asked himself, echoing Walter's question from before. "To show how powerful He is?"

Jack held his hands up in front of his eyes and turned them over, searching for some sign of strength and control. They looked the same as they had this morning, liver-spotted and frail with just a touch of arthritic swelling in the joints. Hardly hands suited for a killing.

Jack turned toward the main house and saw two large male nurses running toward him with what looked like medication and restraints. He noticed with some wonder and detachment that his hands were red with Walter's blood, and that the air seemed unnaturally foul, like something had died recently and been left to decay. But he didn't think much about it. He was too numb to think.

"Don't move a muscle, old man, or we will seriously hurt you," said the nurse with the syringe and the vial of sedative.

Still in a state of shock, Jack was too weak to put up much of a fight. Instead, he turned his eyes toward Heaven for one last glance at what he had tried to save. The sun glared down at him from a cloudless sky, making him squint. Heaven was nowhere to be seen. Jack quickly felt his legs go numb, and he collapsed onto the lawn of the rest home, wondering where his mind had gone and when it had left.

He began to cry as he realized that he had just murdered his only friend in the world during some fit of dementia brought on by old age. There was no blazing hole in the sky, nor were there angels up there recovering from some unseen battle. There was only his mind unraveling on itself, and the frayed ends of sanity that remained.

One of the nurses grabbed him tightly by the arm, but it wasn't really necessary. Jack didn't put up a struggle. The chess board and Walter, meanwhile, sat quietly where he had left them. The chess board was buried under a drift of bloody feathers.

Jack, meanwhile, was a tangled mess of confusion. Knowing that he would need it eventually, he asked one of the orderlies for a shot of whatever was in the syringe. The man gladly administered the tranquilizer. Soon Jack felt his eyes grow heavy from the drugs, and the world became obscured through bloody, confused tears. Feathers fell all around him, soft and pure like snowflakes, and the sky remained clear and bright. It didn't make sense, but then, God never proclaimed to subscribe to human logic. It was a good thing Jack had learned to accept that long ago or else his psyche might have crumbled beneath the weight. Of course, he had also learned that God was just, and he tried to keep that in mind as he speculated about all that he had seen and done.

Although he hadn't put up a fight, one of the orderlies wrestled a set of restraints over his withered shoulders while Jack listened for the sounds of rejoicing in Heaven. There were no such sounds. He did, however, hear Walter screaming out in pain from somewhere beneath the earth. Jack said a prayer for him and scrunched his shoulders together a little to ease the pain in his wings. Had they been there all this time?

Slowly they began walking toward the main house. A single drop of blood fell from the sky and Jack smiled weakly at the orderly, reassured for the briefest of moments that he wasn't senile. The drop landed on the orderly's forehead where it burned and sizzled like acid, yet the orderly looked at Jack as if oblivious to the pain. Then, much to Jack's dismay, he smiled back.

That was when Jack began to scream. And to pray.

THE SMALL HOURS

I t was a little past three in the morning. Normally, Jantzen wasn't even conscious at that hour. In most cases he was either sleeping off his drunkenness on the studio's couch, or he was sleeping it off in a cheap hotel room with whoever he had been able to pick up at The Zodiac. The only reason he had broken from routine tonight was because there were some maintenance and repair jobs at the radio station that needed attending to, and fewer people listened in the middle of the night. Which meant that in case something went wrong, and the station went off the air, no one besides Scary Larry, the late-night DJ, would know the difference.

The maintenance work had been routine, and Jantzen was done with the majority of the tasks in a couple of hours. Normally he would have been anxious to finish his work and hit The Zodiac Club while a few people were still sober and ready for a good time. But things had changed a lot lately. He was beginning to realize that he wanted more out of life than hangovers, cocaine highs, and cheap women.

Not really sure what he wanted to do or where he wanted to go at such a late hour, Jantzen decided to get in his jeep and drive along the coast, hoping that the soothing hush of the waves might ease his mind. As he approached the familiar section of town that eventually led to The Zodiac and the life he was so quickly trying to break free of, he nearly slipped back into his old habits like a worn-out suit, turning on Wilshire when he should have kept going straight. He had been down this road enough times to know what lay at the end, and he didn't want to go there on this particular night. So, he made himself drive right past the street that would take him to the bar, to the flashing lights, to the easy women, and somehow, he felt better for it.

Letting the jeep carry him where it wanted to in the dark night, Jantzen turned on the radio, purposefully tuning it to a station other than WHVY, the one he worked for. In his present frame of mind, Jantzen didn't want anything to remind him of the way he lived, the way his life had turned out. He just wanted a little noise to tear away the silence and boredom and monotony that was blanketing him like a chrysalis. As he had expected, there were a couple of nasally-voiced DJ's who sounded like they were stuck in puberty. There was also the obligatory voice that was so deep it shook the rearview mirror when the volume was turned up loud enough.

But what he hadn't expected was the breathless alto of Alexis, the host of a late-night talk show called The Small Hours.

"Hello out there," she whispered, sending a chill up Jantzen's arms. "These are The Small Hours, and it's my job to make sure that you don't spend them alone. I've got the answers to all of your problems tonight. All you've got to do is listen. Sounds easy enough, doesn't it?"

Jantzen nodded his head eagerly, wondering why he had never heard of Alexis or The Small Hours before. In his mind, he could instantly picture the sort of looks that went with the smooth, tempting voice which seemed as thick and warm as molasses oozing out of his Bose speakers.

"Wouldn't it be nice not to worry about anything anymore?" Alexis' voice lulled like a gentle ocean current. "To break free of the routine you've lived for so long? To escape the mundane life you've been stuck with?"

It sounded like a fantasy to Jantzen, but one that was worth hoping for. He was forty-five, unmarried, and the director of a radio station that nobody listened to; and quite frankly, he was dissatisfied with the way things had turned out for him. He was tired of having to go to The Zodiac every night to find a willing woman, and just as tired of drowning his sorrows in booze when there was no one at home to share his problems with. He had hoped to make something more out of his life, and yet, here he was, driving in his jeep, waiting for revelation, some divine word from above that might give him some sense of direction. And yet it was Alexis, not God, who told him what he wanted to hear.

"Things don't have to be the way they are now," she whispered gently into hundreds of cars and homes across the city. "You and I have the power to change destinies."

Jantzen snatched a pen out of his shirt pocket and quickly wrote down the frequency of the radio station he was listening to on the back of his hand. Whatever he did, he didn't want to forget where he had heard the first voice to ever give him hope.

"I imagine there are some of you who hate your job," she said gently.

Jantzen nodded his head, feeling a little disoriented in the suddenly cramped car, but not really caring.

"Some of you haven't found the person who will make you happy for the rest of your life."

Jantzen nodded his head again and looked wistfully out the window at the waves lapping against the beach. The bottom of the ocean seemed like a peaceful enough place, and he couldn't help but wonder if anyone would miss him if he went there.

"I'm sure there are even more of you who are sick of routines that never satisfy. Booze, drugs, sex. Anything to fill the void. You've tried it, and it hasn't worked."

Jantzen nodded for the third time, thinking that it was extremely uncanny how accurate this woman was about everything. He had snorted everything but paint thinner over the years, and had even considered that option when desperate. His liver was probably pickled given the enormous quantities of alcohol he had consumed at various bars around town. And there weren't many women in Valley Falls who hadn't shared a bed with him at one time or another. Still, he felt empty, like the bottle of Johnny Walker he left sitting on the table each and every Saturday night.

But maybe, just maybe, this woman could help him. His head felt a little woozy with the thought. Still, he tried to shake it off, not wanting to miss a moment of what Alexis had to say.

"You've got to take chances in life," she went on like a commencement speaker. "Do things you would have never thought of doing before. Live your life like you were someone else. Do what they would do."

It sounded like a good idea, and he was determined to heed the advice.

Although Jantzen tried hard to convince himself otherwise, he knew exactly where he was going as he wound through the city. One way or another, he was going to find Alexis, offering up whatever dubious excuse might carry him the twenty or so miles to Crowley's Point. It sounded a little stupid when you said it out loud, and that's precisely the reason Jantzen didn't. This seemed like the only chance he had to break free of the chains that bound him to Valley Falls, his job, his weekly rituals, and he wasn't about to pass it up. If nothing else, driving to Crowley's Point was one of the most spontaneous things he had done in quite a while, and it undoubtedly meant that he was capable of change. But he wouldn't have ever taken the onramp that connected to the interstate if it hadn't been for Alexis. Every word out of her mouth brought him one step closer to change, and that deserved some gratitude.

At that moment, Jantzen felt like he owed his life to her.

"Everyone is dissatisfied at one point or another," Alexis continued mystically, sounding like a cross between a motivational speaker and a shaman. "Me included. That's what brought me to the mainland. I used to live on Gold Hook Island, hoping that every day would be different, that something would happen to change my life. And it didn't. At least, not until I took charge of my destiny and moved to Crowley's Point. I was tired of the routine, the longful waiting, the expectations that were never met.

"So, I looked for somewhere else to go, some place where I could realize those dreams that I didn't even know I had. Undoubtedly, that dream was radio. But how could I have known? Before I moved here, I had never even been inside a radio station before much less worked in one. There were a few people on the island who told me that my voice was a gift, that it had the power to influence people. I suppose I must have realized this at one point or another, but I had never considered it until I saw the flashing lights of the radio station late one night and thought, 'Hmm, that place could change my life.' I couldn't help but think of the people I could reach through the power of the airwaves."

Jantzen pressed a little harder on the accelerator with each of Alexis' encouraging revelations. Not really sure how it would help his cause, but wanting to try anyway, he turned on his cell phone and dialed the number that Alexis had given them at the beginning of the show. For the first five minutes, the line was busy. Jantzen must have hit redial well over a hundred times, but he was determined to get through.

Finally, Alexis answered the phone. "You're living in The Small Hours," she answered. "But you're not alone." The quiet hush of the water and Alexis' hypnotic voice was enough to make Jantzen drowsy. But it was also enough to instantly put him at ease about everything in his life that wasn't right.

Normally, Jantzen wasn't at a loss for words, but for some reason he found that he couldn't say anything.

"I know it's hard to talk about these things sometimes," she added gently. "But tell me exactly what it is you're upset about."

Jantzen took a deep breath, debated for a moment, and then spoke.

"I'm forty-five years old, and I've done nothing with my life. By now I should have gone to Paris, Rome, London, and seen all the things I've heard about. But I was content to stay here and dream. I should have settled down with a wife and started the family I always imagined I would have. But I always convinced myself that I wasn't the sort of man who could ever commit to a woman that deeply. I should have pursued my interests when I went in search of a career. Instead, I settled on something that was comfortable, something I wouldn't have to work too hard at to succeed. Eventually, all my dreams reached a plateau, and I stopped dreaming. When that happened, the routine set in, and now, I don't feel that there is any way out. I'm a man trapped in the everyday. There are no mysteries left for me to explore, nothing new to hope for."

"You sound very depressed," Alexis said with what sounded like a hint of sorrow in her voice.

"I wasn't when the night started out," Jantzen replied. "But then when my work was done, and I was confronted with the same alternatives that I'm always confronted with, I couldn't help but feel like I had wasted my life."

"Yes," Alexis responded noncommittally. "And you're looking for a way out."

"Every day of my life."

"You really should talk to someone," she said sympathetically.

"No one seems to understand but you."

"Then come and talk to me."

Jantzen's foot pressed heavily on the accelerator, and the jeep sped into Crowley's Point in a flash of headlights and a blur of chromed metal.

Although he couldn't explain it, it seemed like everything Alexis said was right on the mark, and he was anxious to know her thoughts on a solution. She knew his feelings, his emotions, his thoughts. And it was a little bit scary. Still, he found that the jeep knew only one direction and that was the one which led to WXXZ.

Within a minute or so of entering the city limits, Jantzen's cell phone rang, and he quickly hit the receive button, hopeful that Alexis was on the other end of the line.

"Where you at, bro?" Larry said in his usual disc jockey voice that was full of the phony excitement and personality that rarely showed up outside the radio station. "I thought you were coming back."

"Something came up, Lar."

"You went to The Zodiac, didn't you?" the DJ asked, just the slightest hint of concern creeping into his voice.

"Nope. I'm tired of being the sort of guy that everybody can predict. I want a life, not a screenplay that can be read once and recited night after night."

"So, where you been, brother? Don't keep me in the dark."

"I'm headed to WXXZ," Jantzen said quietly.

"Is this a joke?" Larry replied.

"No. Why?"

"WXXZ's been closed for almost a year now."

"Well, they're on the air," Jantzen said.

"If somebody's broadcasting from that place, they're doing it without the FCC's permission," Larry protested. "Actually, I'm surprised there's anything coming out of that place. I would have thought the owners would have sold all of the radio equipment to pay for their debts."

"Maybe they've re-established themselves," Jantzen suggested hopefully.

"Then why haven't you heard about it?"

"I didn't know they shut down to begin with," he protested. "They never were a direct source of competition for us. They catered to a different audience and had a different format than we did. I never really did that much research on them, and I haven't had a reason to since then."

"Are you out trying to replace me?" Larry asked coldly.

Normally, Jantzen would have tried to explain himself, reassuring Larry that his job wasn't on the line. But not tonight. No matter what happened when he got to the radio station in Crowley's Point, Jantzen was fairly certain that he would never work at WHVY again, and thus, didn't care what Scary Larry thought. That was why he hung up on him.

He had only been to Crowley's Point a handful of times, but he was reasonably familiar with where the radio station was. At this time of night, there wasn't much traffic, and Jantzen gunned the motor through a couple of yellow lights, his eyes growing wide at the sight of the large billboard with the station's call letters on it.

When he pulled into the WXXZ parking lot with a squeal of tires and a gritting of teeth, he was surprised to find that it was full of cars, all vacant at this time of the night. The radio station facade, however, was neon and bright like an uncovered lamp in the darkness that has attracted automobiles instead of curious insects; and it wasn't much of a stretch to assume that everyone was inside.

"They must be having some sort of party," Jantzen said to himself, dreading those first few steps that would take him into the building. Normally, there were only a couple of people working in a radio station at this time of the night, and Jantzen had assumed that he would have some time alone to talk with Alexis when her show went off the air. Now, it seemed, he was going to have an audience, and that wasn't really something he was looking forward to.

He stepped out of the jeep calmly, hoping he was doing the right thing as the gravel crunched under his feet like brittle bones. He noticed that many of the car radios were still blaring the soft, soothing voice of Alexis, the vehicle headlights piercing the darkness like weak eyes straining to see in it. A few of the cars close to the street had been left running with the keys still in the ignition. Maybe it wasn't a party after all, but for the life of him, Jantzen couldn't fathom why so many people would have stopped to run in for a few minutes and leave.

That was when he noticed the Impala at the front door.

Unlike the rest of the cars parked on that strip, the Impala's interior lamp glowed weakly in the darkness like a candle that has nearly been snuffed. Jantzen peered in curiously and saw by the dim light that the car was out of gas. He listened to the steady rumble of V6 engines in the night and wondered how long the Impala had been left running outside the radio station's front door before it ran out of fuel. Because he didn't want any of the people inside to see him and think he was prowling, Jantzen carefully crept around to each of the other cars nearest to the building and peered through the drivers' side as best he could. Because WXXZ was so well lit, he didn't have any trouble seeing that every one of those automobiles had run out of gas as well.

What is going on here, he thought to himself.

Then he heard one of the cars backfire, like a shot-gun blast in the darkness, and the sound was familiar to him. Searching feverishly through both pockets, Jantzen was surprised to find that he had left his keys in the jeep, and what was more, he had left it running. Strangely enough, however, he didn't care. All he was worried about at the moment was finding Alexis and giving her the keys to his broken-down life. If anyone could get it jump-started, he reasoned to himself, it was definitely her.

The jeep backfired again for the second time, like a cannon blast, and Jantzen nearly considered going back to shut off the engine. But then he heard Alexis, speaking softly from the open win-dows of the cars that were still running, and scarcely even remembered he had a jeep.

"Lives aren't static," she said in a voice that was as even and smooth as the rhythm of a hypnotist's pocket watch. "They don't have to remain set in concrete."

Jantzen forgot all about the jeep. His hand was reaching for the front door before he even realized it. Because there were so many cars outside, Jantzen had expected WXXZ to be buzzing with excitement when he went in. But he was surprised to discover the place in utter disarray. Cobwebs clung to the corners while dust bunnies scurried across the floor. Doors that led to control rooms and offices hung helter skelter in the frames, like brittle bones about to rot away. Aside from the neon sign with the radio station's call letters, the hallways were dimly lit, mostly by single bare bulbs scattered across the ceiling.

It hardly looked as though anyone had been inside the place in months, and yet there were dozens of cars outside. Something wasn't right, but Jantzen was so desperate to talk to someone about his problems that he didn't care. Besides, there was something enchanting about Alexis' voice that he couldn't quite put his finger on which was why he felt like he had to do whatever it took just to hear her again.

Jantzen headed toward the door at the end of the hallway and nearly slipped when his foot hit a streak of something slick and wet. Once he made certain that he wouldn't fall again, Jantzen examined the spot on the floor a little more closely and found that the dampness was actually a trail that led all the way down the hall, ending at the door of his destination.

He raced ahead, making sure to walk on either side of the wet slick that looked like something an overgrown snail might have made. Then he had his hand on the door, and that's when he heard the wet, sticky sound on the other side of the door, like boots trudging through swampy muck, the mud sucking at the leather with each step.

He opened the door and found the room almost entirely dark save for the intermittently blinking lights of a control panel and a mixing board. A pane of heavily tinted glass separated the sound booth from the rest of the room, which prevented Jantzen from seeing very much of Alexis. Yet, even with all the shadows and the poor visibility, Jantzen could tell immediately that he had been wrong about everything.

For starters, Alexis was not the petite woman he had imagined her to be. Her girth was a huge amorphous silhouette on the other side of the dark glass, and he couldn't help but be reminded of those steamy phone sex operators and the overweight housewives they so often turned out to be. Holding his breath, he swiftly turned around, planning to walk out of there like nothing had happened.

But Alexis knew he was there.

"You're finally here," she said, her voice changing timbre a little. At this point, Jantzen felt like he had no choice but to face the woman and explain the terrible mistake he had made. But then he felt something slither up one leg of his blue jeans, and things didn't seem quite so clear-cut. Crying out,

Jantzen jumped and turned to see what had him. Much to his dismay, a long, snaking tentacle was inching its way beneath the cuff of his Levis. Jantzen jerked his leg away in disgust and watched the tentacle snake its way back under the door leading to the sound booth.

Knowing that it was pointless to try and run now that he had been seen, Jantzen pressed his face to the tinted glass and tried to catch a glimpse of the grotesquely fat woman that was undoubtedly waiting for him on the other side. Although it had frightened him at first, he was sure that the serpentine flagella hadn't been what it seemed. But he didn't really have any other explanation that could clear things up.

Trying hard to remain calm, he had nearly summoned his courage enough to open the door and face the woman. Then a new batch of calls came in, lighting up the switchboard in a flurry of red and green blips, and that was just enough to reveal what looked like moist green flesh.

"What the—" he said, snatching his hand away from the door.

In the half-light of the radio booth, he glimpsed the thing that had lured him here with its voice and its promises of a better life. Scary Larry had been right about this place. It had been shut down, and something had seized upon that opportunity to get what it wanted, what it needed to stay alive. Something that hadn't found what it desired on Gold Hook Island.

The air from the control booth stank of decay and excrement, and just the faintest tinges of spice lingered on the air like the smell of something cooking. It nearly made Jantzen's stomach turn, but he managed to keep what liquor and food he'd had down for the time being. Bones picked clean by tentacles and teeth lay heaped in piles around the room, and Jantzen wondered how many men had met their fate here, thinking only of metamorphosis while the siren sang her song over the airwaves, luring breakfast, lunch, and dinner with the enchantment in her voice.

But the thought was short-lived. The tentacle came back with a vengeance, and this time it brought reinforcements. The door was thrown open, and Jantzen's legs were jerked out from under him causing him to strike his head on the hard, concrete floor. Immediately, the creature was on him, all teeth and unblinking eyes and slime, bloated like a corpse that has been sitting out in the noonday sun.

And then his life finally changed as he'd always hoped it would while the siren continued to sing and lure and kill.

PYRO

The Shadow Brothers' Carnival of Chaos was in town, and the night was filled with possibilities. The air was alive with fire, excitement, and the delighted screaming of children. The mouth-watering smell of steamed hotdogs and buttered popcorn was mixed with the wild scents of animals, wet hay, and smoke. Vendors were busy hawking their wares to every kid that passed by in hopes of getting their parents to spend some extra money on balloons, clown noses, and cheap toys that would be forgotten about the next day. Gaudy, painted clapboard signs were set up to announce performers like Aqua the Water Weaver, The Pretzel Man, Mephisto, Thunderbolt, and Fortunato the Clown.

Yet, it was Pyro's tent that stood out above all others. The tent would have been just as brightly lit even if there hadn't been any spotlights.

Pyro looked like a medieval dragon standing confidently in the center ring, exuding smoke from his nostrils. The crowd cheered as he swallowed a flaming torch. He followed it with another and still another until it seemed as if his tongue would be parched and blackened beyond all recognition. He stuck it out confidently, showing the healthy pink of undamaged muscle. The crowd cheered even louder.

Knowing what the people really wanted, Pyro walked over to the front row of seats and spit a massive fireball into the air above their heads. After all the flames he had eaten in the course of his act, this new trick seemed a little like regurgitation. But the people loved it, and that was all that mattered.

With thick clouds of smoke still bellowing in his lungs from the fire eating, Pyro blew a smoke ring that impressively morphed into a set of hazy lips as it wafted through the air. As intended, the smoky kiss landed on the cheek of a beautiful blonde in the front row that he had been eyeing for the better part of the night.

Blushing from the heat and the gesture, the blonde quickly scribbled something down on a sheet of paper and handed it to Pyro. He took the phone number eagerly even though the scrap turned to ash beneath his red-hot touch. This only seemed to excite the blonde even more.

Pyro took it as a bad sign, but he wasn't going to give up just yet. Maybe this one was different.

Playing to the crowd, he reached out his hand

to touch the beauty's long silky mane. Pyro began to get his hopes up when she didn't resist. However, the stench of singed hair swiftly crushed every prayer of ever being with her. This woman wasn't strong enough to withstand his touch. She was like all the rest. Still, he wanted her badly, regardless of the outcome.

"Meet me at my trailer in an hour," he whispered. She nodded, and he smiled before launching another fireball into the hot carnival air.

***

Jeremy watched the woman's reaction to Pyro's performance and knew that the fire-eater could help him get Kara's attention.

He waited until Pyro had finished his act before approaching him. Up close, Pyro smelled like something that had been in the oven for too long. Jeremy wrinkled his nose at the smoky stench and cleared his throat to get Pyro's attention.

"Jeremy," Pyro said, popping a throat lozenge into his mouth. "Something you need?"

"Do you ever get used to smelling like the head of a burned match?" Jeremy asked.

"After a while," Pyro said as he wiped the sweat from his brow. "The bad breath, the digestion problems, the burns. It's all part of the job."

"You get burned?" Jeremy asked in disbelief. "You're supposed to be a professional. That would be like a singer forgetting the words to his song or a chef leaving out ingredients."

Pyro smiled at this. His lips were cracked from the intense heat. "There's not a professional fire eater alive who doesn't get burned on a regular basis," he said. "Any of them that tell you differently are lying."

"Could you teach me how to do it?" Jeremy asked as the crowd booed to show its displeasure. His father, the ringmaster, had just announced that the acrobats wouldn't be performing because one of them was sick. In reality, one of them just hadn't shown up for work.

Pyro stopped to listen to the unhappy throng of spectators for a brief moment before turning his attention back to Jeremy. "This isn't a hobby," the fire-eater said. "This could be a matter of life or death if you don't do everything correctly."

"I don't care," Jeremy said. "I want to do this."

"Why?" Pyro asked. "You must have a reason, and I don't think it has anything to do with following in your father's footsteps as a carnival performer."

Jeremy shrugged his shoulders. "Kara—"

Pyro cut him off before he could finish. "This is not a neat little trick you abuse to get a woman's attention. This is a serious skill that can hurt or kill if you're not careful."

"It obviously works for you. I saw that woman give you her phone number."

"Good. Then you also saw just how much use I got out of it when it burned up in my hand."

"That was just a trick," Jeremy said. "You've probably got it hidden away in one pocket or another."

"I'm not teaching you how to do this as a way to get a date."

I could talk to my father about you," Jeremy threatened.

"Do you realize that this is my job?" Pyro said. "I can't afford to do anything that might jeopardize my place with The Shadow Brothers."

"I'm serious about this," Jeremy said. "I want to learn to do what you do. That's the only thing that will get Kara's attention. Everything else I've tried has failed."

"I'm afraid not," Pyro replied. "The only people your father answers to are The Shadow Brothers themselves, and he can do lots of things to make my life hard."

"So can I," Jeremy said. "I've seen a lot of women go into your trailer. But I haven't seen too many of them come out. Is that something I should bring up?"

Pyro's cheeks filled with fire, and for a moment, Jeremy was certain that he was going to get smacked in the mouth.

"You've been watching me?" he roared. "What else have you seen?"

"It doesn't matter what I've seen," Jeremy replied smugly. "What matters is when our first lesson on the art of eating and breathing fire begins."

Pyro stroked his red beard and tried to regain his composure. For once, he was thankful for the overbearing calliope music. He could say what he wanted to without anyone hearing.

"Regardless of what you've seen or think you've seen, the answer is still no. I won't be blackmailed into doing this."

"There must have been a time in your life when you decided to learn how to breathe fire. Somebody taught you, didn't they?"

Pyro looked at Jeremy with something that might have been pity. "My story isn't as clear cut as that. I didn't choose to work with fire. I inherited it. My father was a fire-eater too. He hated it just as much as I do."

"So that's it?" Jeremy asked, fuming. "That's the last word on this matter? You absolutely, positively will not show me how to breathe fire?"

"Absolutely, positively. No."

"We'll see about that," Jeremy muttered as he walked away. "We will definitely see."

***

What he saw, however, wasn't what he expected to see.

A few jugglers were tossing knives to each other not too far away from Pyro's trailer. One of them raised a hand in greeting to Jeremy but was still quick enough to catch the meat cleaver that was racing toward him. Not wanting to seem suspicious, Jeremy waved back. Then he walked around to the back of Pyro's trailer where he wouldn't be seen.

Carefully, he pressed his nose to the window and looked inside. The blonde from the front row was bound and lying on Pyro's floor. In order to prevent everything from catching on fire inside the trailer, Pyro had lined the walls and floors with silver fire-retardant sheeting, giving the interior the look of a spaceship. Jeremy could hear the crinkling sound of the metallic material beneath the woman as she squirmed and writhed.

The fire-eater looked at her hungrily, and for a moment, Jeremy was sure that Pyro was going to do something lecherous to her. But then he turned away from the woman as if contemplating his next move. The look on the fire-eater's face was clearly one of indecision. Jeremy considered that to be a sign of weakness.

"Please understand I don't want to hurt you," Pyro said. "I just want you to be different than all the others."

Jeremy could hear the woman begging for her life as Pyro hadn't bothered to gag her. It seemed he was trying to be as humane to her as he could be under the circumstances. That made Jeremy think of Kara. He hadn't been nearly as chivalrous with her.

"Please don't hurt me," she said. "If you just let me go right now, I won't tell anybody. We can just pretend this never happened."

"You'll run away."

"What do you want me to do," the woman asked. "I'll do whatever you want."

"All I want is to be able to touch you without hearing you scream."

"I would have let you touch me without going through all this," the woman said, bewildered. "After all, you invited me to your trailer, and I came willingly. Force wasn't necessary."

"You don't understand," Pyro said. "Being with me is different. It's never a pleasant experience. Women always scream when I touch them."

"You can't be that bad," the woman said, hoping that her cooperation would be the very thing that saved her life. "If it's burn scarring that you're worried about, don't be. I'm a paramedic. I've probably seen worse. And best of all, I'll be quiet."

"I want to believe that," Pyro said. "But I can't take any chances. Please forgive me. I'll remove this if it turns out that you're actually capable of enjoying my company." The woman's eyes went wide as Pyro stuffed a gag in her mouth. They got even wider when he grabbed her upper arms with the intent of pulling her closer to him. Smoke seemed to rise off her skin where his fingertips touched. It was a little like watching raw meat being thrown onto a hot grill. She squealed and groaned and grunted as Pyro tried to hold her tight. But he knew that this one would be no different than any of the others, and he let her go. When he released his grip, it looked like someone had tortured her with a branding iron.

"I know you probably think I'm sadistic," Pyro said. "But I'm not. I'm just not like other men. I'm a man of fire, and my touch burns. You can see how that might be problematic in a relationship. But I've tried to be hopeful. I just keep praying that I'll find a woman who doesn't turn to ash beneath my fingers. I was hoping you might be the one."

The woman tried to speak through her gag, but

all that came out was indecipherable groaning.

"It's hard to keep my urges under control," Pyro explained to her. "There's just nobody strong enough to provide for me. I'm destined to be alone."

Even with the gag and the tears streaming down her face, the woman managed a commiserating smile. "Thank you for smiling," Pyro said as he removed the gag and leaned in to kiss her.

The woman opened her mouth to scream, but the sound had no time to rip its way out of her lungs. The fire that leapt from Pyro's mouth was ravenous and all-consuming. Her skin quickly crackled and burned like old parchment. Her bones shriveled from the heat and turned to a dark dust the color of spent gunpowder. Sighing, Pyro swept up what was left of the blonde off of the silver fire-retardant floor and threw her remains in the trash. Then he screamed in frustration.

Unfazed by what he'd seen, Jeremy waited a few minutes before knocking on the fire-eater's door.

"Don't even bother asking me again," Pyro said once he realized who it was. "I've already explained to you that I won't do it and the reasons why."

"Sure, I know," Jeremy said. "But that was all before I saw you incinerate a woman with a kiss."

Pyro tensed at the mention of the dead woman. "You have no proof," he growled. "Besides, it's like they say in detective movies. No body, no crime."

"I'm not interested in jamming you up. All I want is to learn your secret," Jeremy explained, looking around at Pyro's trailer. "Is that too much to ask? Besides, if I turned you in, who would teach me how to breathe fire?"

"I still don't understand why you think that learning how to eat fire will impress Kara," Pyro answered.

"Who said anything about impressing her?" Jeremy asked. "Come. Follow me. I'll explain."

Pyro wasn't sure what Jeremy was talking about, but he did as he was told and left the metallic confines of his trailer. Jeremy walked calmly to his car and popped the trunk. Then, he moved aside so Pyro could see. Kara the Acrobat lethargically climbed out. Jeremy helped her by jerking on the thick length of chain that was wrapped around her delicate, bruised throat.

"What are you doing?" Pyro hissed. "Are you crazy? How long have you had her in there?"

"I want to teach Kara a lesson," Jeremy said. "I want to show her what it feels like to be shunned."

"Let's go back inside before someone sees us," Pyro said.

"Suits me," Jeremy said as he yanked on the chain, eliciting a wounded yelp from Kara. "It's probably best we go someplace fireproof for what I have in mind anyway. Your trailer is just the place."

Pyro sighed. "I think I know why the acrobats didn't perform tonight."

"And I think it's time you showed me what I want to know," Jeremy finished.

"So, she turned you down for a date," Pyro replied, watching the young girl with obvious concern. "Big deal. You have no idea what it's like to be shunned."

It was clear from the way Kara looked at Pyro that she was hoping he would help her escape from Jeremy. Jeremy, however, kept a firm grip on the chain that was wrapped around her throat.

"It is a big deal," Jeremy said. "I want to get her attention. I want to burn her face to the point that nobody else will desire her. Then when she comes crawling to me for affection, I can give her the boot like she did to me."

"Let her go," Pyro said. "Take your rejection like a man."

"Why? You didn't let that woman from the crowd go. You just burned her to a crisp."

"Our situations are very different. Fire is a part of me. It's not something I can teach you."

Jeremy looked around the room again. This time he noticed the pictures that hung on the walls.

In one photograph, an old white-haired man was holding a straightened wire coat hanger that had been loaded up campfire-style with marshmallows. His other hand was aglow with flames.

"That your dad?" Jeremy asked. "The guy roasting marshmallows with his fingers?"

"Yes," Pyro said. "He could do the same things with fire that I can do. I inherited my gift from him. Like I told you before, I didn't exactly choose to be a fire-eater. The job sort of chose me."

"Show me how," Jeremy said. "Otherwise, I'll tell what I've seen."

"How can I teach you the secret that's embedded in my cells?" Pyro growled.

"You'll figure out a way," the boy said, pulling hard on the chain. Kara yelped and looked at Pyro almost pleadingly.

"This is going to turn ugly if you insist on taking it further," Pyro said.

"I'll tell what I've seen."

"No one will ever believe you," Pyro argued.

"I'll make them believe me," Jeremy threatened.

"Despite how hard things have been for you, I don't think you can say that you've endured the torments I've had to endure. You have no idea what it's like not to be able to touch another human being without hearing them shriek and moan in pain. You have no idea what it's like to fall in love with a woman and then watch her turn to dust in your bed. You think you have it so bad, but you don't. There are plenty of other girls to pursue. Why do you have to have her?"

"Enough with the sob story," Jeremy said. "I want to burn this girl, and I want to burn her now."

"I'm sorry," Pyro said gravely. "But I won't be a part of this."

"Have it your way," Jeremy said at last with a sigh and a shrug of his shoulders. "You won't teach me the art of fire. That's fine. I'll just cut her instead."

A look of alarm crossed Pyro's face as Jeremy pulled the hunting knife from his belt.

"No," he screamed as Jeremy brought the knife up to Kara's cheek. Pyro grabbed the boy's wrist, and immediately the crematorium stench of burning flesh was thick and pungent. Pyro barely even winced at the odor. It was something he had grown accustomed to. What he hadn't gotten used to, however, was the screaming.

Jeremy shrieked like a bottle rocket as he flailed around the room. Flames licked up his body like the tongues of insatiable lovers. Even in his agony, he still held on to the knife that he had planned to cut Kara with. Unable to withstand the pain of burning any longer, he plunged the blade into his own chest and fell to the floor.

Aghast, Pyro stared at the burned, lifeless remains of Jeremy. How had things spiraled out of control so quickly? Unsure of what to do next, he did the only thing that made sense and fire-retardant blanket over what was left of Jeremy and sat down in the wrought-iron lawn chair he used in lieu of an office chair. He buried his head in his hands and took several deep breaths. He needed to relax, to think things through.

Unsure of what to do in such a strange situation, Kara walked over to the fire-eater. She started to put a reassuring hand on his shoulder before remembering what had happened when he touched Jeremy.

Pyro smiled at her. A glimmer of hope filled his eyes for a brief second.

"I'm sorry about all of this," he said as he pulled the gag out of Kara's mouth.

"Why should you be sorry?" Kara said, smiling. "If anything, I should be thanking you. You saved my life."

Pyro blushed. "You missed your performance," he said.

"I'll make the one tomorrow night," Kara said. "Because of you. Is there anything I can do to thank you properly?"

Pyro's face twisted with indecision. He couldn't resist the urge. "A little kiss," he said, reaching for Kara before she could escape.

Kara screamed the moment their lips touched, but the noise of the circus and the roar of the fire quickly drowned the sound out.

Pyro's were screams of protest. In his quest for love, he had unwittingly done what Jeremy had meant to do in hate.

The world just wasn't fair.

For Pyro, the fire-eater, the nights would never be lonely and cold.

Lonely, yes. But never cold.

THE MISUNDERSTOOD

Today was the day for fashioning men out of old clothing and hay. Today marked George and Cynthia's fourth year on their rural Thornmire County farm. As annual tradition dictated, George was supposed to build a scarecrow to commemorate the move from city to country. But he didn't really see the point. None of the other three scarecrows had done their job. The carcass in the back pasture was proof of that.

George kicked the mutilated bull with his boot, stirring up a cloud of flies. "Son of a gun," he muttered, running a hand through his thinning gray hair. This was the fifth cow he had lost in less than two weeks.

George suspected the backwoods cult that was rumored to practice in the surrounding woods. They probably sacrificed his cow to Baal or Dagon or Marilyn Manson or whoever it was the kooks worshipped these days. The strange thing about it all was that he never heard a sound during the night.

No chanting. No animal noises. Nothing.

He left the carcass where it had fallen, and walked out into the cornfields to clear his head. The tall stalks swayed and danced in the sun. A ragged scarecrow clad in orange flannel hung from a makeshift cross in the center of the field. It was the one he had made the first year they had bought the farm. There was something almost martyr-like in the way it hovered above the corn like a thief on a cross.

George wasn't impressed.

"A lot of good you've done for me," he said, spitting tobacco juice at the scarecrow. "If you were any kind of a scarecrow at all, my cows wouldn't be dying."

He looked out at the vast expanse of country-side and saw the three scarecrows all hanging there, doing absolutely nothing to stop the loss of his herd. It was all he could do not to rip the strawmen down and set fire to them out of sheer frustration and rage. The loss of those cows meant a loss of money, and money was scarce. He was already be-hind on the mortgage and the note on his tractor. He couldn't afford to keep waking up and finding the remains of his animals lying about the yard. He had to do something.

Over breakfast, he pretended to read the newspaper while he silently pondered his problem.

But Cynthia wasn't fooled. "Something's bothering you," she said as she fed Wyatt, their ten-month-old son.

George put down his paper and sighed. "I found Thunderhead this morning. The body was pretty mangled."

Cynthia frowned. "Have you called the Sheriff yet? We can't keep losing cows like this."

George frowned. "The Sheriff don't care about us. He's got bigger problems than dead cows. This is my mess to deal with."

Leaving his half-finished plate behind, George stood up from the table and walked into the living room. He came back with a twelve-gauge shotgun and a handful of shells.

"Where are you going?"

"To have another look around," George said. "I'll be back after awhile."

He completely avoided the bull's remains on his way out to the woods. He didn't need to see the lengths of wet ropy intestines, or the open windows of striated muscle again to realize that immediate action had to be taken.

Although it hadn't rained in a couple of weeks, there was a very definite set of tracks leading away from the bull's carcass toward the woods flanking George's cornfields. The warm summer breezes had ruined many of the tracks, rendering them un-readable. Yet the direction was clearly defined, and he had little trouble following the marks in the dirt.

The tracks went about a quarter of a mile into the woods, across sun-dappled ground, through a dense copse of elms, finally stopping at a campsite. George was immediately confused by what he saw, but he wasn't exactly sure why. Everything had the look of ritual to it just as he had imagined. The ground was littered with leaves and what looked like dried blood. Strange symbols had been carved into the trunks of the surrounding trees as well as scrawled in the dirt.

George had seen most of this before and wasn't really bothered by it. Misguided teenagers dabbled in the occult all the time and found this particular stretch of wilderness a good place to practice. Mostly, they just stared at the stars around a campfire and recited incantations in Latin. As far as George knew, the incantations never amounted to much. The teenagers were usually drunk when they wandered out here in the first place.

This, however, felt different. The intricacy of the symbols and the copious amounts of blood was part of it. The enormous crater in the earth the size of an SUV was the other part. George studied the gigantic hole with fascination and trepidation. He wasn't an expert on this sort of thing, but there was one thing that made him doubt the hole had been made by a meteorite. There, at the edge of the hole, was a set of massive handprints that gave the impression that someone or something had clawed its way out of the earth.

Hoping to get to the bottom of everything, he decided to spend the night on his porch. The vantage point from the porch gave him a clear view of all his fields. If something happened out in the corn patch, he would see it...and stop it.

Dark fell quickly. The sun melted into the horizon and was replaced by the moon which looked cold and frigid. The wind blew just hard enough to make lighting a pipe difficult. George finally managed to keep a match burning on the third try. Smoking, however, didn't have the same effect that it usually did. His nerves were wound tight like guitar strings, and he just knew that something was going to happen at any minute.

When something did finally happen, however, it wasn't at all what George expected. He had just closed his eyes for a moment when he heard the shrill sound of crows cawing in the fields. Something had disturbed them.

He opened his eyes to see the scarecrows, one by one, coming down from their crosses to head toward the house.

The pipe fell from George's open lips, but he hardly noticed as the smoldering ash spilled out onto the porch. His attention was focused on the ragged hay-men that were striding through the corn rows toward him. The shotgun suddenly seemed like pitiful protection.

George would have stood his ground if the threat had been a mountain lion, a wolf, even a grizzly bear. He knew those things, recognized them for the danger they represented. The scarecrows, however, didn't fit into his nice, tidy perception of the world. They should have still been hanging there in the corn fields, repelling the magpies. But they weren't.

In earlier times, scarecrows were used to ward off evil spirits along with the worrisome birds. But now, it seemed as if the scarecrows were possessed by the very evil spirits they were designed to repel.

Quickly, George sprang up from the rocking chair and raced inside the house. He took the steps two at a time.

"Cynthia, wake up," he said sharply as he entered the room. "Get Wyatt."

Cynthia sat up immediately. "What's wrong?"

"Just get Wyatt and go into the attic."

Cynthia saw the shotgun in George's hands and

nodded. It only took her a few seconds to grab baby Wyatt and scramble up the ladder to the attic. George followed quickly behind her, pulling the ladder up.

He put his finger to his lips in a quieting gesture, then he crept cautiously toward the window. He didn't see the scarecrows, but he heard a struggle of some sort going on outside. He couldn't tell what was happening, but it sounded like the scarecrows were trying to break into the house. He heard something thud against the outside wall, followed by the shattering of glass.

"They're coming inside," George hissed. "Keep the baby quiet and don't say a word."

Cynthia nodded.

They waited for what seemed like hours. George wanted to run to the window and see what was going on, but the plywood floor was sure to creak if he moved too much.

He looked at his watch and waited for five excruciating minutes. He expected the fiends to bust in on them at any second. He expected to hear them scrabbling around on the roof. He expected one of them to jump through the window.

But none of that happened. Not even after ten minutes.

Cautiously, George motioned for Cynthia and the baby to stay put. Trying hard not to put too much weight into each step, he carefully tiptoed to the attic window. He took a deep breath, checked his shotgun to make sure the safety was off, and peered out, surprised by what he saw.

The scarecrows were all in their rightful places, hanging from makeshift crosses in the cornfields.

"I don't believe it," he whispered. "The scarecrows don't look like they've moved."

"Scarecrows?" Cynthia asked.

"They were walking around out there."

Cynthia crept over to join her husband. "The scarecrows look just like they always have," she said, a hint of worry creeping into her voice.

"I'm not crazy," George protested. "I saw them coming toward the house. Something broke the downstairs window. It didn't break itself."

"I'm sure there's a perfectly good explanation for it all," Cynthia said.

Realizing that there was no point in arguing, George dropped the attic ladder and climbed down. "Pull the ladder back up," he said. "I'll let you know when it's safe to come down."

"We'll wait for you," Cynthia replied. "Be careful."

It was a little over five minutes before George returned for his family. "The window is destroyed," he said, obviously frustrated. "Come and see for yourself."

When they got to the window, hundreds of bits of broken glass crunched beneath their feet. A thin pool of spreading black gore puddled beneath the windowsill.

"What is that?" George asked, disgusted.

"It's blood," Cynthia said. "Animal blood, I would imagine."

"Animal blood?" George questioned.

"You probably just thought you saw those scarecrows coming toward the house," Cynthia rationalized. "What you saw was a wild animal charging at you, and the scarecrow was situated in the background. You probably just transposed the two and imagined you were seeing a scarecrow."

"No," George protested. But it was a very weak protest. Maybe everything had happened just the way she had described it.

"I think we should go to bed now," Cynthia said, obviously relieved now that the threat had been confined in her mind to something that a rifle or a bear trap or another natural predator could take care of. "This has been a long day. We're all exhausted. Wyatt's starting to get cranky. You're tired. We all need some rest."

George couldn't argue any more. He couldn't even argue the fact that the scarecrows had been alive. The truth was, he wasn't sure.

He spent the next few minutes out in his workshop, digging out a sheet of plastic and a roll of duct tape. He used them to cover the broken window in hopes of discouraging animals from making themselves at home in his living room. Then, he lumbered to bed, his mind full of questions.

Surprisingly enough, he slept soundly. When he woke up, he was hopeful that the events of the day before were just a big misunderstanding. He realized that wasn't the case, however, when he went outside and found another dead cow, mutilated like the others.

The carcass, by itself, wasn't much of a surprise. What he hadn't expected was what he found in the folds of dead, fly-infested meat. In another place, it would have seemed harmless, inconsequential. But here in the rank, steaming bowels of a cow, the blade of hay was completely out of place. If nothing else, it reaffirmed George's belief in what he had seen the night before.

This time he didn't give Cynthia the chance to rationalize the situation.

"I want you to take Wyatt to your mother's for tonight and let me handle this."

"We're not leaving you," Cynthia said. "Call the game warden. Tell him what's going on. I'm sure you're not the only one who's losing livestock.

Maybe somebody's reported seeing a cougar or a pack of wolves."

"I can take care of my own house and my own land," George erupted. "What I can't do is take care of the threat and take care of you at the same time."

"George—" Cynthia began.

George cut her off short. "Just do what I'm asking you to do," he said as sternly as he could.

She nodded and quietly headed to the back of the house to prepare for the trip. It took her less than an hour to pack a few of their things and load their son up in the car.

George breathed a sigh of relief as he watched the Honda drive away.

The moment he was certain that they were gone, he started his preparations for the night. He gathered up his shotgun, extra shells, a pair of binoculars, a can of kerosene, a pack of matches, an axe, a sling blade, and a pitchfork. He wasn't sure what good any of it would do.

Once or twice he grabbed up the can of kerosene and the pack of matches, and he set out toward the fields to burn the scarecrows before they got the chance to crawl down from their perches and wreak havoc. But he always stopped short of the fields, scared and more than a little unsure of himself. The scarecrows didn't move except when the wind tousled their flannel shirttails or rustled their pants legs. They looked too ragged and incapable of movement to be any real danger. Maybe something else had been coming at him from across the field. Maybe Cynthia had been right about what he had seen.

He sat on the porch all day long. He kept his eyes on the fields, searching for the faintest sign of movement on the part of the scarecrows. The strawmen, however, were still.

By the time the sun began to dissolve like a piece of orange candy, George was tired and frustrated, and growing more and more certain by the minute that he had been mistaken.

Then he heard the cows snorting and kicking up dust in the field behind the house. Cursing, he grabbed his shotgun and ran around the porch to see what was causing so much commotion.

Everything looked as it was supposed to at first glance.

Everything except for the dead cow.

George knew that whatever had killed the cow had done it in seconds. Of course, the scarecrows couldn't have done it. He'd had his eyes on them the entire time.

Yet, he wasn't even certain of that anymore, as when he ran to the front of the house again and found that all of the scarecrows were gone. The sling blade, the pitchfork, and the axe were gone too.

George pumped a shell into his shotgun, grabbed the kerosene and matches, and ran back around the house, fully expecting to see the scarecrows murdering one of his cows in cold blood. The scarecrows, however, hadn't reached the cows yet. But they were headed in that direction, brandishing the axe, the sling blade, and the pitchfork like rioters in a Frankenstein movie.

"Stop," George screamed at the scarecrows, temporarily distracting them from their mission.

The gaunt figures turned to look at him with their black button eyes.

George dropped the kerosene and matches and raised the shotgun. The first shot nearly cut one of the scarecrows in half. George pumped the shotgun again and was about to fire a second shot when the scarecrows turned from him and headed toward the cattle. They were lithe like cats, and the shot missed by a mile, disintegrating one of the fence posts.

The can of kerosene and the matches lay useless at his feet. Weighing his options, George decided to discard the gun and to go with fire instead.

Unwilling to get too close to the scarecrows, George ripped a swatch of cloth from the tail of his work shirt and stuffed it into the mouth of the gas can to use as a fuse. Then he lit the match. The cloth was old and dirty and caught fire easily. It was all George could do not to hurl the can immediately, as he was terrified of the inevitable explosion. But he willed himself to count to five before launching the can of kerosene into the air like a pot of boiling oil from a catapult.

The kerosene can exploded in midair, sending smoldering fragments of metal and a heavy rain of fire down on the scarecrows and the cattle. The cows' skin was tough and had endured similar marks from branding irons before. The fire seemed to almost slide off their leather backs.

It wasn't nearly so kind to the scarecrows. One of them, the first one George had ever fashioned, blossomed into flames like a white-hot flower. It flailed and flopped around like a beheaded chicken for several seconds before finally collapsing in a smoking pile of burned hay and cloth.

Satisfied with his progress, George was just about to finish what he had started and hunt the last scarecrow down when he saw another set of eyes lurking at the edge of the murky woods surrounding the corral. The scarecrow, pitchfork brandished high, had stopped and seemed on the verge of attacking the threat in the woods. But attacking what, George asked himself?

His question answered itself as a shadowy, blood-soaked behemoth with glowing golden eyes stepped out of the forest to face off with the scarecrow. It was like no animal George had ever seen, and he knew immediately that this was the beast that had emerged from that pit he had stumbled onto at the ritual site. This was the beast that someone had called forth.

With that realization came another: He had been wrong about the scarecrows. They weren't responsible for the deaths of his cattle. The scarecrows had done as they were made to do, attempting to scare away any threat to the farm. He had just been too stupid and unobservant to realize it. To make matters worse, he had completely decimated two of the strawmen, leaving only the one to defend itself and the farm.

The lone scarecrow was no match for the dark juggernaut.

George watched in horror as the fiend picked up the scarecrow and ripped its legs off like the wings of an insect. The scarecrow, however, wasn't going to go down without a fight. It buried the pitchfork deep into the yellow eye of the beast as the scarecrow was tossed away like a rag doll.

The same sort of black blood that George had

seen near his broken window oozed out of the beast's wounded socket.

The beast howled, sending the cattle into a frenzy. But the fence that corralled them was electrified, and the cattle knew better than to get too close. The juggernaut, however, did not. It smashed through the fence as it rushed at George. The voltage-drenched wire sparked and sizzled where it touched demonic flesh.

George grabbed his discarded shotgun off the ground and fired a quick succession of shots. The fiend was much too strong and much too fast. The buckshot bounced off it like pebbles off a speeding freight train.

George turned to run but knew that he didn't stand a chance of escaping. Whatever had been called forth out there in those woods was much stronger than any weapon. It was also much faster than George.

Twisting his ankle, he fell beside the remains of the Holstein that had been killed only minutes before. He winced at the smell of exposed innards. Hobbling to his feet as the dark, brooding entity from the woods gained ground, he saw something out of the corner of his eye that surprised him as much as anything possibly could at this point. The scarecrow he had cut in half with the shotgun was pulling itself toward him, hauling itself forward with one arm, brandishing the axe in the other. Staggering along behind it was the smoldering remains of the badly burned strawman, sling blade hanging limply from its grasp. The scarecrow whose legs had been ripped off was dragging itself toward the fight as well. What was left of the three scarecrows was all that stood between the demonic horror and George.

Knowing that he would fall again if he looked back, George set his sights on the house and moved as quickly as he could. It would only be a matter of seconds before the beast was upon him. Yet strangely, even after a few seconds, George found himself alive and still moving toward sanctuary.

Gasping, he reached the front door. Flinging it open, he staggered inside and hobbled over to a window. He watched as the beaten, dismembered scarecrows used every last ounce of strength to corral the dark, horned beast. Although badly charred, the burned scarecrow held up its crippled brother so that it could ram the pitchfork's tines into the monster's glistening head. The demon howled in pain as the pitchfork pierced its skin and bone. The scarecrow that had been cut in half by the shotgun blast hacked away at the creature's legs with the axe.

The strawmen weren't as strong as they had once been, but they were resolute in their defense of George and his house. Wounded and angry, the beast staggered drunkenly around the field with a mighty roar, but not before grabbing two of the scarecrows and flinging them into the corral with the cattle who quickly trampled all over the remains. Bleeding profusely from its wounds, the beast stumbled and fell toward the third scarecrow, who managed to raise the pitchfork before being crushed beneath the demon's weight. The fiend screamed once as it fell onto the tines of the hay fork. A dark stream of blood ran from its wounds, scorching the earth and the scarecrow beneath.

George watched it all in amazement as the fiend seemed to dissolve right before his very eyes. Soon, there was nothing left of the beast but a patch of burned ground and a few charred bits of hay.

The monster was dead. The scarecrows had killed it.

George still didn't know exactly what he'd witnessed, but he knew he was fortunate to be alive. Whatever had been summoned forth from the bowels of the earth was gone now, and hopefully, he could get back to the business of cattle farming.

George smiled weakly. It was the first time in two weeks he'd been able to manage such an expression.

Wincing at the pain in his ankle, he hobbled

from window to window, watching for several minutes to make sure that the threat was over. Drained from two solid days of vigilance and edgy nerves, he collapsed into the recliner, relieved that the threat was finally over. He could rest easy for the first night in a long time.

And then he realized that he couldn't really. There were still things left undone.

With a sigh and a tired smile, he got to his feet and lumbered to his bedroom to pull out some old clothes. Before he went to bed, he still had a few scarecrows to make.

This time, he thought to himself, I'll make them twice as big.

Just in case...

THE CHASE

Nights in Valley Falls were mysteries to be solved. Each of them held cryptic messages to be uncovered, unraveled, and mulled over. The nights harbored secrets, and sometimes if you listened hard enough, you might hear one whispered on the wind.

Tonight was exactly the sort of night for learning things.

Spader had just sat down to a hot cup of coffee when his cell phone rang, echoing in the silent diner like the toll of a church bell. This late at night, it could only be bad news.

"What is it?" he answered around a mouthful of soup and crackers.

"We've got a multiple homicide on the boulevard," Gibson said. "If you want to see it before the chief arrives, you'd better get here quick."

"Any details?"

"For starters, the body count is four. A family. And you wouldn't believe how ugly it is. Blood everywhere."

"What's the house number?"

"I don't know the address," Gibson said. "But you'll see the flashing lights."

"I'll be there in five."

Gibson, dressed in his officer's uniform, met Spader at the front door of the house. With a quick flip of the wrist, he flashed his credentials at the policeman who was standing watch.

"You two go on in," the officer said weakly. "But I'll just tell you up front, this crime scene ain't pretty. Whoever did this is certifiable."

Gibson nodded his head in agreement and led the way to the dining room.

The family was seated at the dinner table. They had been in the middle of eating bowls of vegetable soup when the killer struck. The mother sat at one end of table. The father sat at the other. One child—a boy—sat on one side of the table. His sister faced him. All their throats had been slashed. The table and the floor underneath it were a sticky red mess.

"Their hands are tied, and their ankles are bound to the chairs," Spader said, wrinkling his nose in disgust at the heavy smells of blood and meat. "How original."

"The killer held them at gunpoint long enough to subdue them," Gibson replied nonchalantly.

"Probably made the father tie up the rest of the family, and then, once they were all cozy, the knives came out."

A lab technician with heavy latex gloves pulled one head out of the swirling red muck of blood and vegetable soup long enough to discern that the victim's throat had been slashed.

"Nasty cut," Spader said detachedly, having seen a bit of his father in that face. With their heads nearly severed, and their bodies partially drained of blood, the dead family brought back lots of memories, reminding him of the way his own parents had looked at the scene of their murders.

Ever since he was six years old, Jack Spader had been fascinated by murder scenes. It was at that age that his parents had been butchered by the Havenwood Slasher before his very eyes. Right before it all happened, Jack had been hiding under his parents' bed, reading one of his father's secret magazines when he saw the killer nonchalantly slip out of the closet like a shadow.

There, beneath the bed, Jack loitered in Flash Gordon pajamas that were a size too small for him. His Buck Rogers laser pistol was fastened securely to his hip. The magazine was spread in front of him, and the women smiled at him from the glossy pages like friends. Having never seen anything quite like it before, he didn't notice the closet door swing open, or the man with the blood-red eyes stand statue-still in the darkness. For all intents and purposes, the world could have blown up around him, and Jack wouldn't have cared in the least. He and his crew were elsewhere, on a planet where the women walked around, unclothed and laughing. There was no need for a gun in this place. These natives were friendly.

The illusion was shattered when Jack heard the killer take his first step.

Jerking his head out of the magazine, afraid he had already been caught, Jack nearly banged his head on one of the bed rails. But then he saw that it wasn't his father, and the decision to be relieved or terrified wasn't as clear cut. The knife that the man carried, however, helped him quickly make up his mind. Not knowing what to do, he instinctively drew the laser pistol and stared at it stupidly, completely forgetting the magazine. He almost fired the gun before remembering the high-pitched whine that it made. That would attract attention for sure. So, he holstered it fearfully and held his breath, hoping the big man with the knife couldn't hear his heart as it threatened to beat its way out of his chest.

In retrospect, he knew that he should've warned his parents about the killer who was walking down the hall, but he was too afraid that his father would find out what he had been doing under his bed. So he did nothing. In the end the cuts were quick and messy and to the bone. Blood spurted in thick viscous pools across his mother's shiny new linoleum, spreading outward in amorphous circles. He remembered how his mother always complained about him tracking mud across her recently waxed floor with his cowboy boots, and he hated himself for not preventing such a mess. All it would have taken was the squeeze of a trigger. Buck Rogers would have been ashamed of him.

When Jack finally summoned the courage to check on his parents, Louise Spader was hauling herself across the slick linoleum with badly lacerated arms, her face as white as fine porcelain. The bloody pool chased her vigilantly, growing larger as she grew weaker. Jack remembered hugging his bleeding mother to his chest as the light fled from her eyes.

The shiny chrome pistol at his side had never been fired, and his mother's blood covered the floor as a result. Even now the hot tears burned his cheeks as he remembered her last breath hitting him in the face like a furnace blast. He had turned away to keep from crying in front of his father. Jack Sr., however, had been crying too, wiping his face with the back of his bloody hand before facing his son.

Not wanting to seem cowardly in front of his father, Jack drew his gun.

"Don't worry, son, death makes slaves of us all," his father murmured as he took his last breath. Jack held the gun stupidly in his hand for a moment, at last flinging it into a corner, sobbing because he hadn't done more to help.

Spader thought of that now and was reminded of his self-appointed mission. Ever since he had seen death as he truly was—a sallow-faced man with acne scars and needles marks on his arms—he had vowed to track him down and kill him. But he seemed to be no closer now than he had been ten years ago. It was a depressing thought.

Luckily, the sound of a camera shutter opening and closing brought him back from his nightmare.

It was Gibson, furtively taking picture after picture. "There might be clues here," he always insisted, knowing full well that the chief would blow a piston if he ever got wind that one of his men had snapshots like this in his possession. But Gibson was careful, never taking more than a few photos at a time before stashing his phone in one of his pockets. Spader tried not to question Gibson's actions. After all, if it weren't for him, he would never have gotten as close to the bodies as he did. Still, Gibson repulsed him sometimes.

"Our boy's definitely crafty," Gibson said with admiration. "And he certainly knows his way around a blade."

"Yes," Spader replied. "It looks like our man."

"And he's so versatile," Gibson went on.

"You sound like a fan," Spader said smugly. "How droll."

Gibson mouthed an obscenity under his breath and leaned over to inspect one of the killing wounds. "The cuts aren't clean. He didn't do it in just one stroke. He probably used a serrated knife. And a dull one from the look of it. Something that had to be sawed a little to make the cut."

"Do you get off on this?" Spader asked, not really wanting an answer.

Gibson looked hurt by the question. But he took another picture before he answered.

"Funny," he said, "that you should be asking me that. After all, I'm not the one who's been using the fortune his parents left him to chase a killer around the country. You hired me to get you into these sorts of crime scenes, remember? I'm not the one who has turned one traumatic incident into his life's work. I'm not the one who—"

"I get the point," Spader said bluntly, sorry he ever brought the subject up.

Although it was hard to tell with so much blood

in the room, the man Spader was looking for had definitely been here. No doubt, he might look nothing at all like the killer who murdered his parents twenty years ago, but it was the same animal, vicious and cruel. His mark was on the place like a bloody fingerprint, and Spader had no doubt that the trail was still warm. But he didn't have time to find it.

In the distance, Gibson heard the labored sound of the chief's beat-up sedan approaching from down the street. As if to confirm it was him, the sedan backfired twice. Quickly, Gibson pocketed the camera and pushed Spader toward the door.

"I'm not even on duty right now," he hissed. "If the chief sees me, he'll wonder why I'm here. And there's no telling what he might do with you. Which means we should go. Now."

Gibson ran to his cruiser and went in the direction of the Lamplight Theater while Spader got in his jeep and drove toward the hills to think and calm down after everything he had seen. While he drove, the trees passed on either side of him like a smearing of green and ocher paint, and, for a brief moment, Spader wished that he could forget everything he had ever seen and replace it with memories of nature. But then he saw the natural world at work as a vulture swooped down to dine on a dead squirrel lying on the side of the road, and he changed his mind, realizing that brutality was simply a part of life.

As he watched the vulture tear the flesh from the fly-laden carcass, Spader couldn't help but think of Gibson, snapping picture after picture, taking advantage of the dead. Undoubtedly, the vulture was the more honorable of the two. After all, it was his nature to prey on the dead.

His phone rang, not giving him the chance to finish the thought.

"We've got a suspect," Gibson said with some enthusiasm. "They've found a fingerprint. Jarrett Reed is the guy's name. A Social Studies teacher at the elementary school. They're scouring the area for him even as we speak. But that's not even the best of it..."

According to Gibson, another handful of victims had been found in the basement of a well-respected minister. Strangely enough, although the tragedy seemed unrelated to the dinner table murders, the victims' throats had also been slashed. It reminded Spader of animals sacrificed to a demanding god.

Gibson texted him the address, and Spader quickly headed to the crime scene.

For the first time in his life, Spader didn't want to see the bodies. He didn't want to see the slaughter or listen to the maddening click of Gibson's cell-phone camera. All he wanted to do was to forget everything he had ever seen and give up the chase. But it wasn't that simple.

"These incidents are connected," Gibson remarked over the phone as he drove. "I'm sure of it. I don't know how yet, but we will figure it out. This guy has been busy. It's impressive in a weird sort of way. Don't you think?"

"Say what you want about him," Spader said dryly, having heard enough. "Call him a genius. Point out over and over again how clever he is. Put him up on a pedestal with The Zodiac Killer and Jack the Ripper. But when you peel away the flesh to see what makes him tick, you won't see the brilliance. All you will see is a sick, decaying mind, and a sociopathic disposition. Not a man with guts, just a man who is too insane to care about getting caught. A sad man. One to be pitied as he's strapped into the electric chair."

Gibson, however, heard none of this. He had hung up.

Spader skidded the jeep to a stop near the minister's house with a crunch of gravel and a cloud of upturned dust. Gibson was already on the move, jumping out of the car as if he were on fire. Spader noticed that he had brought his camera with him and was loading it frantically as they walked toward the front door.

"Where is everybody," Spader asked, noticing that the driveway was empty save for Gibson's Monte Carlo and Spader's own jeep.

"I haven't notified them yet."

Spader looked at Gibson, his eyebrow arched in concern.

Gibson held his hand up to stop Spader. "Old Lady Hartwell lives next door. When I was younger, she used to be our housekeeper. Seemed more like an aunt than anything else. That was why she called me. Said she hadn't seen Reverend Packard in several days. Apparently, that was unusual because he always collected her newspaper for her and brought it up to the porch before he went to his church. She said she's had to collect her own paper for the past three or four days. Today, she got worried enough to knock on his door. When he didn't answer, she went in to check on him, thinking he may have had a heart attack or something. And then the smell hit her."

Spader was all too familiar with the stench of death. It wasn't something he wanted to experience again tonight, but Gibson was insistent.

"I checked the house and found the bodies," Gibson continued. "But I knew this was something you might want to spend a little more time on than usual. I guess we just got lucky on this one."

Spader looked at Gibson with disgust at the mention of the word 'luck.' For the moment, he didn't need any more of Gibson's schoolboy enthusiasm. Especially not after he saw the victims lying in a pool of blood in the basement.

Although he had seen a lot in his time, Spader had never seen anything quite like this, and he took a minute to compose himself.

Gibson, however, walked over to the heap of bodies and knelt beside one of the female victims. The flies had already begun laying their eggs in the open wounds of her throat.

"So where is Reed in all of this?" Spader asked, having composed himself enough to speak.

"Don't know. The school said he hasn't shown up to teach his Social Studies classes in two weeks. He told them his mother had died, and he needed a little time to get her affairs in order. Because he's such a well-respected man around the place, people hardly questioned the explanation."

"And the minister?"

"Doing missionary work in Belize or someplace like that. He's been gone now for over a week, and just didn't bother to tell Mrs. Hartwell. Which means everything still points to Reed. Apparently, Reed attends Packard's church on occasion. He must've known that the reverend was going to be out of the country."

"How convenient," thought Spader.

The victims were heaped together, arms draped over arms, legs draped over legs, heads lying together as if they were joined like Siamese twins.

"I'd better call this one in," Gibson said with some regret. "Are you about finished?"

Spader nodded. He didn't need to see anything else.

Within fifteen minutes, the patrol cars had arrived along with a squad of ambulances. Spader watched them from a reasonable distance down the street. Gibson hadn't wasted any time leaving the scene of the crime, and Spader knew that he should have been long gone too. But he felt the need to watch them take those bodies out of that dreadful house, and pray for their souls.

Although he hadn't really meant to, Spader had left the police band radio on in his Jeep after talking to Gibson. As it crackled and hissed, he turned it up, hoping to hear someone expressing the slightest sign of grief over the loss of so many innocent lives. Instead, he heard one officer declare that they had found what looked like the decaying body of Jarrett Reed at the bottom of the pile. Even stranger still was the fact that Reed seemed to be missing one of his fingers.

"Cut right off at the knuckle," was how one of the officers described it.

Within seconds of the news, Spader's phone rang.

"Reed didn't do it," he said, knowing it was Gibson before he ever heard the man's voice.

"How do you know that?" Gibson asked hesitantly.

"Because they've found his body."

"Interesting. That changes things a bit. But I'd be willing to bet a kidney that whoever killed those kids and that family is the same person responsible for offing the teenage couple I've just happened upon."

"What is this?" Spader asked in amazement. "A Friday the 13th movie? Where are all these bodies coming from?"

"Who knows? Just meet me at the edge of Miller's woods."

Spader knew the spot; it was no more than a mile away. An easy walk from here. Although he was tired and frustrated, he agreed to meet Gibson in ten minutes. On the phone, Gibson's voice had been uneven with excitement, and something about that bothered Spader. Something about all of this bothered him.

He had hired Gibson to be his inside man, to get him access to crime scenes that might resemble the one he had lived through as a young boy. He had wanted a ticket to the show but, instead, had gotten an all-access V.I.P. pass to a horror movie that was taking place in real time.

It didn't make sense.

Rethinking the situation, Spader re-dialed his associate's number.

Gibson answered promptly on the first ring, his voice full of hope and arrogance. "More bodies?" he asked.

"I'm afraid not," Spader replied. "Just a slight delay."

"What is it?" Gibson asked, disappointment in his voice.

"One of your investigator buddies noticed me sitting here in my car. He just wants to ask me a few questions. But I'll be along in no more than twenty minutes."

The words hung heavy in the air like suicides dangling from their nooses.

"But," Gibson began, his voice dropping a full octave.

"And about these two lovers," Spader interrupted.

"Yes?" Gibson asked, his voice suddenly full of the old vim and vigor.

"Were their throats slashed like all the others?"

"You could say that," Gibson answered

cryptically.

"Ok, thanks. That's what I needed to know. I'll see you in a bit."

Spader started for Miller's woods immediately. The police didn't have any questions for him. But Gibson didn't know that and didn't have to. Spader suspected that Gibson had been playing the same sorts of games with him all along.

He thought of driving and then decided against it. The jeep would be much too loud and would announce his presence long before he arrived. Walking, he decided, was the better alternative; it would allow him the advantage of secrecy.

He started toward the woods while the sun was a deep slice of orange on the horizon.

When he got within a hundred yards of the spot Gibson had described, the sun had turned to black, and the moon had arisen in a sickly white. Spader looked at the illuminated hands of his watch and found that he had a few minutes to spare.

Up ahead, the trees were clustered together, and the shadows were heavy like sludge. The wind was still, and the woods were silent except for a single murmuring voice. It was undoubtedly Gibson, although for the life of him, Spader couldn't understand what he was saying. He crept a little closer, not daring to make a sound.

And then a sight stopped Spader dead in his tracks. There Gibson stood, triumphantly over two dead lovers, a bloody knife in one hand and a camera in the other. The killer backed up a little and held the camera up to his face. Unsatisfied with what he saw through the lens, he adjusted the dead girl's hair so that it didn't obstruct the terror that was frozen on her lover's face.

"Perfect," he said to no one in particular. "Spader will love this."

Spader took a step forward, checking as he went to make sure he still had his gun. He felt the reassuring chill of cold steel against his skin and continued to walk as quietly as he could. He never even noticed the fallen branch in front of him until he heard it snap under his weight. Gibson immediately tucked the knife into his coat, his eyes darting wildly from tree to tree, afraid of what might be watching him.

Knowing that he had been detected, Spader stepped into the meager half-light.

"Oh," Gibson said, relieved, "it's you."

"Yes," Spader replied. "It's me."

"Do you see what I found?"

"I see the mess you've made."

A look of confusion crossed Gibson's face. "What do you mean?"

"All these years I've been searching for a killer, and one has been standing beside me the whole time. Of course, you look nothing like the man that murdered my parents so many years ago. But you're the same brand of monster."

Gibson pulled the knife out of his coat. "You needed me," he said. "I gave you what you paid me for. You needed access to murder scenes. I provided that."

Spader said nothing.

"Without me, your life would have had no purpose," Gibson said as he turned the knife this way and that in the moonlight. "You wanted to look for a killer, and as long as there were fresh bodies, you had some sense of direction. I did all of this for you."

Spader pulled his gun. "I didn't need your help to find my purpose," he said through gritted teeth.

"You did," Gibson argued as he snapped a picture of the dead. "You needed a case like this."

"Is there anything else you want to show me?"

"Might as well let you in on everything," he said, pulling Jarrett Reed's severed finger out of his pocket. "I thought it was pretty clever. Just a few well-placed fingerprints and the chase was on."

"And the priest?"

"He's in the trunk if you really want to have a look."

"Why did you kill him?"

"He's the only person I knew that had a basement. And he really doesn't seem to be the type of guy that would let you stash a couple of bodies for a few days without some sort of persuasion."

Spader held his gun tightly in his hands and summoned his courage, feeling scared like that young boy had so many years before underneath his parents' bed.

Gibson laughed at him and his fears, running the blade over his tongue to taste the fresh blood. "Well," he said. "Now that you've finally caught me, what are you going to do? Call the police and turn me in?"

"I'm going to do what I should have done all those years ago," Spader said.

With that, he became a boy again in his mind, frightened and unsure of himself. The killer before him shifted the knife from one hand to the other and took a step forward. Jack's small fingers closed around the handle of the Buck Rogers laser pistol, and he knew that he was being given a second chance to make right what he had been unable to on the day his mother and father had died. He knew that when he opened his eyes, the slasher would be in front of him, and he took an extra breath to calm himself.

Then, he blinked. And there the monster was.

"Without me," the Havenwood Slasher said, "you'd have gone crazy a long time ago. I gave you purpose. I gave you everything."

Jack Spader, six years old and trembling, raised the laser pistol and aimed.

"Bang," he said as he pulled the trigger. The gun sounded like a cannon this time, not a cosmic light ray, and Gibson hit the ground like a falling rock. Even in death, the smile was frozen on his lips like a mask. And despite what his eyes told him, Spader knew that there was another face under Gibson's—the face of the man who had stepped out of that closet so many years before.

Not only had Spader caught up to his demons, but he'd finally found a way to outrun them.

The chase was finally over.

THE LAST WILL AND TESTAMENT OF LAZARUS GRAY

A s the last story came to a conclusion, Lisa looked around with uncertainty at the other members of S.T.A.L.K. "That's it," she said. "There's only one more thing to read. It's a note on the last page. It says:

'I'm afraid I haven't left you with many clues about which of these stories will actually come to pass. To be honest, I'm not sure myself. My mind is not what it once was. I hope you will figure this mystery out and do some good here. It's all I ever wanted. Oh, there's one more thing. Your organization isn't a charity. It is a business with expenses, salaries, overhead. Those things aren't cheap. I'm asking you to take on cases I couldn't solve. Therefore, I am officially hiring you. I have arranged for all my assets which total around $100,000 to be transferred via wire to your account in return for your services. By the time you read this, the money should be in your account. It may not have looked like I had much, but I was wise with my money. I hope it will be enough for the work you have ahead of you.'"

The note was signed, "Until we speak again, Lazarus Gray."

The four members of S.T.A.L.K. looked at each other with confusion and uncertainty. Mikey popped another unlit cigarette into his mouth and rolled it back and forth from one side of his mouth to the other. Cedric went back to fiddling with his watch again as he contemplated everything he had just heard. Anna stared off wistfully into space, letting her mind wander and her consciousness float free. Lisa kept waiting for someone to say something, to interject, to say it was all a bunch of hooey or that it was something they should definitely investigate further. But everyone was lost in their own thoughts.

None of them knew what to think about what they had just read...or if any of what Lazarus Gray said in his letter could possibly be true. What if all of these stories were fiction and the result of a medical condition that caused a man's own thoughts to become unreliable? The entire premise was madness if you stopped to think about it. And to top it all off, he said he was paying them a hundred grand to tackle all of the cases he left behind in this trunk, with each book containing one tragedy that would come to pass if they didn't stop it first.

Could any of it be true?

Lisa raced over to the computer as a thought occurred to her. There was one way to prove at least part of what Gray had said was true. With a few clicks of the mouse and a flurry of keystrokes, she navigated to the S.T.A.L.K. bank account. "Sweet Mary and Joseph," she exclaimed. "The money is there!"

Everyone raced to look over her shoulder at the computer screen.

"We don't have to worry about how we'll stay in business for the foreseeable future," Cedric said. "This is amazing...and a little bit frightening."

"So, he was telling the truth about that part," Mikey grumbled, fully aware of where this conversation was going. "That doesn't mean the rest is true."

"About that," Cedric said. "Let me recap to make sure I understand all of this correctly. One of these stories is true according to Lazarus Gray, and it will take place sometime within the next twenty-four hours. I have a pretty open mind, but even this stretches things a bit too far for me. How would we ever determine the validity of these stories?"

"We've already proved that he was telling the truth about the money," Lisa reminded him.

"I can't believe I'm actually siding with Mikey for once, but he does have a point. How would we even start to investigate the stories themselves?" Cedric asked. "Don't get me wrong. The money is amazing. But the responsibility is a lot. Anybody else feel differently?"

They all simply stared at one another. The silence grew heavy and oppressive as no one was quite sure how they should proceed.

At last, Mikey spoke up. "Maybe we're making this harder than it really is," he said. "Everybody is online now. Let's look up all the people mentioned in these stories and see if we can figure out if any of them actually exist or not. I would be willing to bet none of them are legit. Just some stories conjured up in the mind of a very sick old man."

"Lazarus Gray wouldn't leave us a hundred thousand dollars if he was delusional," Anna said. "There is a ring of truth to all of this."

"But we still have to check this out," Lisa reminded her. "If it is legit, we have to figure out which story is the true story."

"I know which one is real," Anna said. "The Carnival of Chaos has been to Valley Falls several times. It's real, and it's here in town right now. It's also the thing that was mentioned more than once in these stories."

"She's right," Cedric said. "I've seen flyers up all over town."

"There are two stories in the book that deal with the carnival," Lisa asked. "How do we know which lead to follow?"

Cedric pulled his smartphone out and did a quick search until he found what he was looking for. "I've got The Shadow Brothers' Carnival of Chaos website pulled up here. Guess who is one of the performers? I'll give you as many guesses as you want and will tell you if you're getting hot."

"No way," Mikey said, unwilling to consider what was unfolding before his very eyes.

"Pyro," Anna said with a wry smile.

"This can't be real," Mikey exclaimed. "I can't explain why this is impossible, but you all know it is! We're being set up. I'm sure the carnival posted its schedule months in advance. It would be easy enough to write a story about one of the performers and date it for today."

"But what if it isn't a set-up?" Anna asked. "What if it's exactly what it's portrayed to be? Lazarus Gray believed in his visions enough to leave us a lot of money. That kind of conviction speaks to me."

"It's a lot to consider," Lisa said. "But we're

investigators, so we should do what we're good at and investigate this. If it's a hoax, or if someone is trying to pull a fast one, we need to get to the bottom of it."

"Or, if that story is going to come true and we can help save some innocent lives, we should do that too," Anna added.

"Sounds like we're going to the carnival then," Cedric said. "I could sure go for some cotton candy."

"You always think about food," Anna said with a grin.

"A man's gotta eat," Cedric replied. "Now, let's get moving. We can go in my jeep."

"Let's go," Mikey said. "I'm ready to get this over with. I hate carnies."

***

The first thing they did once they arrived at the fairgrounds was follow Cedric's idea and run an online search. After a cursory scan of the Internet, Cedric was able to find one of Kara the Acrobat's social media accounts. Quickly browsing her photos and posts revealed that she had a sister who lived a regular life and had nothing to do with the carnival.

Cedric googled the carnival's phone number and called the box office. The woman who answered the call listened to what he had to say, and Cedric gave the performance of a lifetime. What he said was enough to get the call transferred to one of the carnival managers. The carnival manager was shocked by what Cedric told him and promised to relay the information quickly.

After five minutes (during which time Cedric managed to find a cotton candy vendor), he refreshed Kara's social media account and was relieved to see a post that read: "Prayers needed please. Just got a call that my sister has been in a terrible car wreck. I'm headed to the hospital now."

"That seemed too easy," he said, proud of his own ingenuity.

"Are we sure about this?" Lisa asked.

"Think about it," Cedric said around a mouthful of the pink gossamer spun-sugar concoction. "With Kara gone, Jeremy didn't have the opportunity to abduct her and throw her in his trunk, which means that she should be safe."

"Don't pat yourself on the back too hard," Mikey reminded him. "You don't know that you saved her life. There's no way to verify if that story would have come true."

"Maybe not," Cedric agreed. "But at least we know for certain that she won't end up dying because of Jeremy or Pyro. At least not today anyway.

As far as that part of the story goes, I just guaranteed that it won't come true."

"That call was pretty cruel," Mikey said.

"Dying would be even worse," Cedric reminded him.

"I don't think she would have died," Mikey said, still unwilling to buy the story.

"Can we just move this along?" Cedric said with a note of irritation in his voice. "It's exhausting having to defend our thoughts and actions to you who always feels the opposite no matter what."

Mikey held up both hands in mock surrender. "By all means. Lead the way, good sir."

Cedric scowled at his friend and headed straight to the firebreather's tent. "You'll believe one of these days," he called out over his shoulder. "I'm sure of it."

The group made it just in time to see the blonde from the crowd give Pyro her phone number, and they watched in amazement as the scrap of paper turned to ash in his hand. Just like in the story, Pyro reached out to touch her hair and drew back as his touch caused a few strands to singe.

"No way," Mikey said. "No freakin' way. This feels like déjà vu."

"Can you explain it?" Cedric asked, fully enjoying Mikey's confusion.

"It's a set up," Mikey exclaimed. "These people are acting out a script."

"Do you really believe that?" Lisa asked him with a wry smile. It was clear she was enjoying his reaction as much as Cedric.

"Not really," Mikey said. "There is a logical explanation. I just haven't come up with it yet. But I will."

"Despite Mikey's disbelief, I'd say we chose the right story to pursue," Cedric said over another mouthful of cotton candy.

"If that's true, then we know what fate awaits the blonde," Lisa reminded them. "We have to stop that from happening."

"You do remember that the guy from the story could start fires with his touch, right?" Mikey said. "I don't really want to get close to him."

"But you don't believe any of this," Cedric reminded him. "So everything should be ok. Right?"

Mikey scowled. It was clear he didn't like having his own words turned against him. "I think we should just leave well enough alone here."

"We don't have a choice," Anna said. "That girl will die if we don't do something."

"Ok, let's say for the sake of argument that this whole strange scenario is real and we have the power to save a life," Mikey said. "Isn't this a little like Back to the Future? Maybe we shouldn't do something that will alter the timeline."

"It's not like that," Lisa said, growing more and more irritated with her boyfriend by the minute. "We didn't go back in time, and this hasn't happened yet. We aren't altering the future. We're creating it."

"When a butterfly flaps its wings in Brazil, it creates a tornado in East Texas," Mikey said. "This could have a ripple effect."

"You're right," Cedric said. "We've already set a chain reaction into motion that will save three people's lives. That's a ripple effect I don't mind. The whole reason we started S.T.A.L.K. was to help people. That's what we can do here. Are you so afraid of being proved wrong that you would risk innocent lives to be right?"

"Ok, fine," Mike said. "Forget I said anything. You three are in charge. I'm just the realist of the group here. I'll go with the flow. How are we supposed to stop this guy without anybody getting hurt?"

"I have an idea," Cedric said. "Pyro's motivation is finding out a way to touch another woman...or to be touched by one. We have two women on our team."

"You want to use one of us as bait?" Lisa said, taken aback.

"Why not?" Mikey said. "We're saving lives. Remember?"

"I'll do it," Anna said.

"Absolutely not," Lisa interjected. Her cheeks were flush with anger as she glared at Mikey. She was furious that her own words had been used against her. "You don't have to prove anything to him."

"It will be fine," Anna said, obviously not concerned about any of that. "But we need to get moving. If the rest of the story is true, Pyro will be heading to his trailer soon. The blonde will be heading there as well."

Lisa wasn't happy with the idea, but it was clear that Anna wasn't going to be deterred. "We'll discuss this later," she said to Mikey through gritted teeth.

"What did I do?" Mikey asked, shrugging his shoulders.

"Let's go!" Anna said. "We don't have time for a lover's quarrel."

The four of them set out immediately for Pyro's trailer, and luck, fortunately, was on their side.

They intercepted the blonde on her way. She was surprised when Lisa stepped out of the bushes to approach her and even more surprised by what Lisa told her.

"Pyro isn't who you think he is," Lisa said. "Did you know he is currently being investigated for murder? He lured me back to his trailer exactly like he's done with you, and I nearly paid for that mistake with my life."

The blonde's eyes grew wide, and after thanking Lisa, she wasted no time heading the opposite direction. Which left Pyro in his trailer by himself. No doubt, he was waiting and wondering when the blonde was going to show up. In Lazarus Gray's version of the story, the blonde was already bound and gagged by now. That much, at least, was different in this version of the story.

"Ok, so we've prevented Kara's death and stopped the blonde from getting burned alive by Pyro's touch," Lisa said. "Without Kara, Jeremy won't have a reason to approach Pyro again. Can we assume he's safe as well?"

"We can't assume anything," Cedric said. "Maybe there is a way to help Pyro with his problem and guarantee that he and Jeremy don't have any sort of interaction."

"And how do we do that?" Lisa asked.

"Leave it to me," Anna said, teasing her shoulder-length blonde hair. "I have an idea. I'm the bait, remember?"

And with that, she walked up to the door of the trailer and knocked while the rest of the team hid in the bushes nearby. Hoping to get back in Lisa's good graces, Mikey pulled out his phone and started filming the entire thing like he always did on other cases.

Pyro opened the door with a smile that quickly turned to a look of confusion when he saw Anna. He had been expecting one blonde and was surprised to see a completely different one.

"Yes? Can I help you?" he asked, stroking the red hairs on his chin.

"I wanted to meet you," Anna said, gushing over him like a schoolgirl. "You were amazing tonight."

"Um…thank you!" Pyro said, taken aback. "Do I know you?"

"Not yet," Anna said. "But that could change quickly. I'm Anna. I just had to meet you. You're so…hot. Sorry for the pun. I know this is terribly forward of me, but would you like to grab some coffee with me? I know a place nearby. I won't take no for an answer."

Pyro shrugged his shoulders. One blonde was as good as another as far as he was concerned. "Sure, why not?"

"Great," Anna said with a playful wink. "Who knows what coffee could lead to?"

"Really?" Pyro said, cocking his eyebrow.

"Of course," Anna said, playing the part. "I'm sure you get this sort of reaction from women all the time."

"Well…," Pyro said noncommittally.

"It doesn't matter," Anna said. "I think you're

absolutely fascinating."

"I'll get my things," Pyro said, quickly darting back into his trailer.

A minute after Pyro grabbed his gloves and coat, the two of them were walking down the path leading away from the fairgrounds. The road was mostly dirt and the occasional patch of scrub. It was worn down from years of cars driving back and forth across it for fairs, circuses, rodeos, tractor pulls, and various other outdoor activities that needed little more than a wide open field to set up shop.

Anna looked over her shoulder once to make sure her friends were still back there. She saw a red flashing light in the bushes from the attachment Mikey was using on his phone, and that was enough to reassure her. The more time they could waste, the more unlikely that Pyro would encounter Jeremy. All she had to do was stall, and time would do the rest.

Only Pyro seemed to have other plans. They had walked a quarter of a mile away from the fairgrounds when he pulled his gloves out and started to put them on his hands.

Anna studied him carefully. "Everything ok?" she asked.

Pyro grabbed Anna by the upper part of her arms. "No, everything is not ok," he said. "These gloves are made of asbestos. They are more for your protection than my comfort. Without them, I would have burned you to a crisp. Now, I'm not an idiot. What is all of this about? I know you're not some starstruck groupie. Who are you really? What kind of game are you playing with me? You aren't very good at baiting innocent men. Did somebody put you up to this?"

Anna sighed, and her eyelids fluttered like the wings of hummingbirds as she caught a glimpse of the future that gave her hope.

In the moment Pyro had grabbed her she had seen something, a fork in the metaphysical road that none of them had thought to take. It was enough to cause her to tell the truth. For the first time since leaving S.T.A.L.K. headquarters, she had a plan that would work.

"My friends and I came to stop you," she admitted. "In a different version of this story, you killed three people tonight."

"Are you crazy?" Pyro asked, looking over his shoulder and scanning his surroundings to make sure he wasn't being set up. "I haven't killed anyone."

"You would have killed that blonde who gave you her number at the performance if we hadn't shown up. She was supposed to come back to your trailer. You would have touched her and burned her alive. She would have been like all the rest. In that version of events, Jeremy kidnaps Kara the Acrobat and comes to you to learn how to torture her with fire. He sees you kill the blonde in your trailer and tries to use that as leverage. You kill him when a fight breaks out between the two of you, and then you kill Kara with your touch when she tries to thank you."

"Who are you?" Pyro snapped. "You're crazy."

"We're friends who want to help if you will let us," Anna said gently. "If you won't let us help you, then I guess that would make us enemies. The choice is yours. Guys, come on out."

"Who are you talking to?" Pyro asked in a panicked voice.

"Guys!" Anna said, louder this time.

Pyro scanned the surroundings and eventually the other three members of S.T.A.L.K. stepped out of the scrub and overgrowth.

"Don't hurt her, please," Lisa said, pleading with the carnival performer.

"You came to me not the other way around," Pyro reminded her.

"We came to help," Anna said. "We know you are unable to feel the touch of a woman. We know how you feel. We know how desperate you are."

"You don't understand what this feels like," Pyro said with a surprising note of pain in his voice.

"You don't know anything at all. All I want is to feel a connection with another human being. Is that so wrong?"

"We don't know what that's like," Cedric said. "You're right about that. But it must be very lonely."

"I'm just tired of being alone," Pyro said. "It's a curse."

"I know how to help you," Anna said. "Will you hear me out?"

"How?"

"I see things," Anna said. "Did you know Madame Ruby?"

"Ruby?" Pyro said, confused and unable to see how she figured into things. "Of course, I knew her. She was a sweet lady. She was the best fortune teller The Carnival of Chaos ever had. Certainly much better than that clown, Amir. Anyway, I hated what happened to her. I considered her a friend."

"Do you remember the ghost hunting group that consulted on the case?"

A lightbulb went off over Pyro's head, and his eyes filled with understanding. "That was the four of you."

Anna nodded. "That was us. I didn't know it at the time, but Madame Ruby was my long-lost grandmother. I found out not long after the case ended. She got in some trouble at one point in her life. That trouble caused her to run off and leave the family when I was just a baby, to join the carnival. Staying on the move was the only way she could stay alive. Nobody understood it at the time, but I get it now. I inherited my gift from her. It was a shock when I learned the truth about all of it."

"So, you're a psychic like her?" Pyro asked.

"I'm not nearly as powerful as she was," Anna admitted. "She had years to hone her skills. With time, I might be as good. But I don't need to be as good as her to solve this mystery. I know how to help you. When you grabbed me, something flashed into my mind. It's a solution that is so simple and so logical that I'm surprised no one else has thought of it before. It will fix everything for you."

"It will?" Pyro asked.

Anna nodded. "It will. Will you trust me?"

Pyro considered it. "Trust you even though you just lied to me?"

"What do you have to lose?" Anna asked. "You hold all the cards here."

Pyro's gaze darted from Anna to her teammates and back again. At last, he released his grip on her. "Don't try to trick me," he said. "You don't want me as an enemy."

"We're well aware," Cedric said. "We read about what you are capable of."

"I haven't killed anyone," Pyro protested.

"And we're determined to keep it that way," Lisa said. "Now, Anna, what do you have in mind?"

Anna smiled. "Follow me," she said. "I know where we can go. There is someone we need to go and see."

This time the group walked together back toward The Shadow Brothers' Carnival of Chaos. They walked through the gates and headed toward the sideshow trailers. The area Anna headed for was reserved for carnies that weren't headliners but still had some odd skill or another that made them valuable to the carnival.

She stopped in front of one particular trailer, pointing at it. A look of understanding dawned on Pyro's face. "It couldn't be that simple, could it?"

"It is," Anna said. "I've seen how this turns out, and the outcome is good."

"I don't know if I can go up there," Pyro said, suddenly shy. It was easy to be confident when you knew the outcome. This time he was doubtful, unsure. This was new territory.

"Trust me," Anna said. "This will work. I'm sure of it."

Pyro nodded and took off his asbestos gloves. He handed them to Anna, and she accepted them eagerly.

"Go ahead," she said. "You can do this."

Pyro's face was pale, and he looked like he was on the verge of being sick. "What do I say?"

"Just talk about anything. Compliment her. That's always a good place to start. Besides, I already know she likes you."

"You do?"

"Of course! I've seen it."

Pyro nodded and walked toward the trailer designated for "Aqua, The Water Weaver."

He looked back at them with uncertainty, like a young man leaving for his first date. Anna waved to him and shooed him onward.

He knocked at the door to the trailer and was greeted by a beautiful raven-haired woman. She seemed surprised to see him, but also delighted that he had stopped by. She offered her hand, and when Pyro took it, nothing happened. No smoke. No fire. No pain. He looked back at Anna and smiled before going into Aqua's trailer.

"Could it be that simple?" Lisa asked.

"Opposites attract," Anna said. "This proves it. Water quenches fire. They are perfect for each other. She's the only one here who can withstand his touch."

"You did it!" Cedric said. "You saved three lives today."

"We did it," Anna reminded him. "And now that Pyro is busy getting to know Aqua, there is no way that he and Jeremy will run into each other. So, no one dies today."

"And what about tomorrow?" Mikey asked. "Jeremy didn't abduct anyone today. That doesn't mean he won't in the future."

"But you don't believe in any of this anyway," Cedric reminded him. "So what difference does it make?"

"I'm trying to stay open minded about it all," Mikey admitted.

"You're trying to get out of the doghouse with Lisa," Cedric laughed.

"That too," Mikey admitted.

"I have an idea about how to ensure Jeremy doesn't hurt anyone at a later date," Cedric said as he pulled out his phone and placed a hasty call. Someone picked up on the third ring. "Yes, I'd like to report an assault at The Shadow Brothers' Carnival of Chaos. One of the performers, Jeremy, assaulted one of the girls. He has a history of it. Please come quickly and investigate it. I'm sorry. My phone is about to die. Remember, Jeremy is the guy you need to check out. Come quick."

And with that, he hung up. The other three stared at him strangely.

Cedric shrugged. "Jeremy has a sadistic streak, if the story is to be believed. He won't do anything if he knows the police are keeping an eye on him. It will make him think twice before doing something stupid."

"Maybe," Anna said. "And that's about the best we can do, I guess. I'm not getting the sense that anything else bad will happen to these people in the future. So maybe we've done what Lazarus Gray wanted us to do."

"We did something positive here," Lisa said. "This feels really good."

"So, what's next?" Mikey asked. "Maybe we start a homeless shelter? Cure cancer?"

"You're such a jerk sometimes," Lisa said. "Can't you just let us have our win?"

"Fine," Mikey said, knowing better than to push his luck again. "But in all seriousness, where do we go from here? It feels like we've been given a mission. A big one."

"Our next move is easy," Anna said. "We grab some dinner and go back and look at those other journals. Thankfully, we will have more time to review the other books in that trunk and figure out which story in each one is real."

"This is really happening, isn't it?" Mikey asked.

"We're going to make a believer out of you

yet," Lisa said.

"I wouldn't go that far," Mikey said. "But I do believe in dinner. On that we can agree."

And with that, the S.T.A.L.K. group closed the book on one of the many posthumous adventures Lazarus Gray would send them on.

The future holds lots of other strange cases for this group of paranormal investigators, but those are stories for another time.

Case closed.

ABOUT THE AUTHOR

Jason Brannon is the author of *The Tears of Nero*, *The Cage*, and many other novels and short story collections. He is also the co-creator of The Deadbolt Mystery Society. His work has been translated into German and optioned for film. He loves horror movies, Sherlock Holmes stories, video games, rock music and escape rooms. While he knows all there is to know about the town of Valley Falls mentioned in this book, he would never live there.

Made in the USA
Middletown, DE
03 September 2022

72056990R00116